TITLE: Two Line 27

TRIM SIZE: 6.0000 X 9.0000

PAGE COUNT: 168

TEXT STOCK: 60# Natural Recycled 360 PPI

COVER STOCK: 12 PT C1S (FSC)

COVER COATING: Matte Film Lamination *smooth*

PRESS: KBA

BINDING: Perfect Bound (Hinge Score)

MISC:

Two Lines Press

EDITOR
CJ Evans

MANAGING EDITOR
Jessica Sevey

SENIOR EDITORS
Scott Esposito
Michael Holtmann

ASSOCIATE EDITOR
Emily Wolahan

EDITORIAL ASSISTANT
Sarah Coolidge

FOUNDING EDITOR
Olivia Sears

DESIGN
Isabel Urbina Peña

COVER DESIGN
Quemadura

SUBSCRIPTIONS
Two Lines is published twice annually.
Subscriptions are $15 per year; individual
issues are $12. To subscribe, visit:
www.twolinespress.com

BOOKSTORES
Two Lines is distributed by
Publishers Group West. To order,
call: 1-800-788-3123

TWO LINES
Issue 27
ISBN 978-1-931883-64-1
ISSN 1525-5204

© 2017 by Two Lines Press
582 Market Street, Suite 700
San Francisco, CA 94104
www.twolinespress.com
twolines@catranslation.org

This project is supported in part by an award
from the National Endowment for the Arts.

ART WORKS.
arts.gov

Editor's Note

Quietly, I'm opening my head and driving the world out.
—Kamil Bouška, translated by Ondrej Pazdirek

It's an old adage that great literature reveals some truth to you. That may be true. However, I feel lately like I spend a lot of time battling a feeling of defeat while trying to interpret what's true in the seemingly endless barrage of "news" from what is, ostensibly, the real world. Certainly, when I was rereading this issue of *Two Lines* last night I paused when a line from Jeremy Tiang's translation of Yan Ge's story perfectly summed up my mood: "If he smiled, he would die."

Two Lines is, as all publishing is—and especially as all international, literary publishing is—a political act. And many of the poems and stories in this issue touch, obliquely, metaphorically, or specifically, on politics from around the world. And that is something we are always trying to do: widen the political perspective by including views from all over the world in this, whether you like it or not, irreversibly globalizing age.

Sometimes, though, I need to separate, to unfasten from the seemingly endless theory and punditry and fact-molding. Sometimes the only way to look ahead is to see neither the forest nor the trees, but to climb up a hill and try to see what's beyond the boundaries of the whole mess. And this issue of *Two Lines* has poems and stories that are no less powerful, no less resisting, and no less revealing by being about an affair, like Ji Yoon Lee and Jake Levine's translation of Kim Min Jeong's "Red, an Announcement," or about caterpillars, like in Simon Pare's translation of Katja Lange-Müller's "A Precocious Love of Animals."

Perhaps it's naive, but I do believe that if I occasionally "open my head and drive the world out," it might just seep back in a little more humbly and honestly.

CJ EVANS

Fiction

Poetry

Essay

VERÓNICA GERBER BICECCI is a visual artist who also writes. Her book *Conjunto vacío* won the Aura Estrada prize for literature and will be published in Christina MacSweeney's English-language translation by Coffee House Press in 2018. Her pieces in other media reflect on the visual politics of writing.

Conjunto vacío

¿Tenía novia? Hecatombe interior. Después de comer, Alonso(A) se levantaba de la silla y me dejaba en la mesa con la promesa de volver, pero tardaba demasiado y Yo(Y) terminaba yéndome a casa. Al principio creí que estaba en el baño, después me di cuenta de que se encerraba a hablar por teléfono. Me armé de valor y le pregunté a Chema cómo se llamaba la novia de Alonso(A). Mayra(M_Y), con *y griega*, dijo sonriendo. Sentí feo porque esperaba otra respuesta. Disimulé. Alonso(A) y Yo(Y) nos contábamos muchas cosas pero no me había dicho nada de Mayra(M_Y).

Esto pensaba:

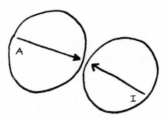

Translated by
CHRISTINA MACSWEENEY

Empty Set

Did he have a girlfriend? Inner cataclysm. After dinner, Alonso(A) would rise from the table, and leave me there with a promise to return, but he always took too long, and I always ended up going home before he did. Thought at first he must be using the bathroom, but later realized he was shutting himself in there to speak on the telephone. Plucked up my courage and asked Chema what Alonso(A)'s girlfriend was called. Mayra(M_Y) with a *y*, he replied, smiling. Had hoped for a different response, and so felt sad and bad, but didn't show it. Alonso(A) and I used to tell each other many things, but he hadn't said anything about Mayra(M_Y).

This is what (I) thought:

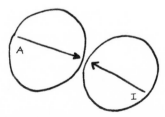

But reality is tough:

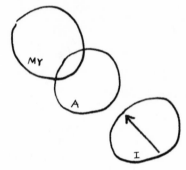

Violeta had been my friend since elementary school, and she was one of the few people I spoke to during those months. She was auditing a class at UNAM that was directly related to her thesis topic. She also spent a lot of time studying in the Main Library for her intensive course in Chinese in the Modern Languages Department; she'd gotten the idea of doing a master's there, but it was going to take her four years just to learn Mandarin. She invited me to go to the library with her because she was worried about me. I had nothing better to do in the afternoons, so accepted the invitation.

She did the talking, I didn't feel up to it, but even then, she'd manage to convert my silence into something pleasant. How did she put up with me? Sometimes her boyfriend came with us too. That was convenient, because it saved me from feeling guilty about not talking. He went to the Aesthetics Library, where he was analyzing a Mixtec or Zapotec (not really certain which) codex for his bachelor's thesis. They used to discuss me. I'd nod, but hardly understood a word of it; suddenly "my situation" seemed to be a pretext for talking about other problems, ones that weren't exactly mine.

Spent the first visits to the Main Library leafing through books, mooching around the corridors, repeatedly going up and down the building from top to bottom, convinced I'd find something, although not quite certain what. In fact, I spent the time imagining a reunion with Tordo(т), imagining he'd repent and come looking for me; going over and over the scene in which he steered me to some out-of-the-way shelving unit and cornered me there, where we couldn't be seen. There was no need to invent a reason for him being in the Main Library, or an explanation for how he knew he'd come across me there. What was important was the reconciliation. These things happen when you've got nothing to do. Then I began to lose hope. Well, in fact, I decided that reunion (of course it never happened) would lack all spontaneity if every single detail of it already existed in my imagination.

It finally occurred to me to look for hypothetical titles in the database. Perhaps someone had already written about everything I needed to know at that moment: *On the Analysis of Time in a Pine Plywood Board*, *Depictions of Time in Wood*, *Grain Lines and Time: A Theory of Chaos*, and other such combinations that, naturally, didn't bring up any results.

When an event is inexplicable, a hole is created somewhere. So we are full of holes, like a Gruyere cheese. Holes inside holes.

A postcard next to my bowl of soup:

Chema had already gotten into the habit of setting a place for me at the table, so I went down at two thirty on the dot. At that hour, Alonso(A) would usually be taking the lids off the pots and pans while chatting to me about what he'd done during the day. It was an invitation to an event at the Museo Tamayo with the pompous title, *The Poetics of the Illegible: Dysgraphia, Hypergraphia, Lettrism, and Other Twentieth-Century Visual Writings*, and was addressed to Marisa(M_x). Despite the fact that the title was so pretentious, and it had a subtitle from a thesis, the idea of attending appealed to me. As he hadn't turned up for lunch on that particular day, it wasn't clear whether or not Alonso(A) was inviting me to go with him. Just in case, I took the postcard with me, supposing that was the best way to communicate my intention.

Translated by Christina MacSweeney • Spanish | Mexico

My routine was pretty simple: get on with my plywood board in the mornings; meet up with Violeta in the afternoons. Sundays were still dinner at Dad's. But Saturdays were dangerous because there was no fixed routine. The first Saturday I decided to leave the house, I ran into Tordo(T). Several weeks, perhaps months, had gone by since I'd moved out. My presence brought the diagram of the triangle into the visible spectrum, even though Tordo(T) denied the existence of that figure. They used to call me sometimes with a request to do the exhibition photography for a small gallery in the Condesa neighborhood. Guess it was cheaper to employ me—an absolute amateur—than to get a professional with the necessary equipment. I arrived early, set up my tripod, and started shooting; the place was empty. Tordo(T) knew perfectly well I'd be taking the photos at some point because he was the one who got the job for me. After a while, I turned around and there they were, coming through the door, arm in arm, like two people who have spent their whole lives together. A three-line space should be left here. It seems to me that formatting could contain a moment of high tension: three and a half blank lines. But that would be giving it undue importance.

Unlike me, photography was Her(H) profession. And from the moment Tordo(T) first met Her(H), he never stopped going on about it. That was suspicious, but I didn't make the connection. It's still not clear to me how a "Someone stole her camera, but she didn't turn a hair, just went on dancing" or "I'm not completely sure about her visual discourse, she's an opportunist" could give rise to mistrust. So it didn't, until that very moment when the two of them were there, across the room, and it dawned on me that he'd never directly introduced us, just pointed Her(H) out from a distance. And it was odd when Tordo(T) insisted, "The haircut the girl had in that video was really ugly." It should have made me suspicious that a woman who clearly wasn't should "look ugly," but apparently, for the first time in my life, I wasn't being a *suspicionist*, and was incapable of seeing the wood for the trees. That's the most awful part of it: something so obvious wasn't.

We have to accept—I wanted to say to them as an icebreaker, but no words came out of my mouth, nothing came out—that if we join the distances between us with straight lines, the result would be more like a triangle than any other figure. The three of us are there, paralyzed. I had time to analyze and measure; it was an isosceles triangle, but slightly deformed: the side joining them was much shorter than the ones they shared with me.

Guess that's the way it always is. Hi, hi. Goodbye, goodbye. They go off set, and I just stand there on the spot, like a tree. The triangle stretches out and out and out, but doesn't snap.

I roundly refuse to form a part of that triangular configuration they are imposing on me. Prefer to think of myself as a cone; some people say a cone is a rotating triangle, all the better. A cone can also be a series of circles tapering from large to small, with the smallest being just a dot. Or a perfect time shaving. So the map of the situation, or rather, the Universe(U) in which (I) was trapped, could be seen differently. What's left of me could also look like a slice of pie. Tordo(T) and Her(H), they're just triangles:

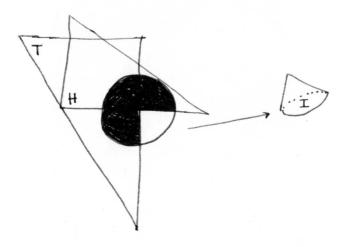

After that encounter, it occurred to me to type just one keyword into the search engine of the Main Library: *triangle*. A book in English appeared: *How Can a Triangle Be Cut?* The title seemed fated, it was exactly what I needed. But the basis of all the solutions to cutting triangles in that text, in addition to being impossible, resulted in other triangles. Wasn't completely sure exactly what I was looking for, but did know more triangles weren't the solution to my triangle problem.

Translated by Christina MacSweeney • Spanish | Mexico

"If only telescopes didn't just look toward the sky, but were able to pierce the earth so we could find them..." says a woman with a small spade in her hand, walking around in the middle of the Atacama Desert. That's how the documentary film my Brother(B) and I saw in a small independent theater starts. She and a number of others have spent decades looking for the bodies of their disappeared. There are enormous telescopes in the Atacama Desert that see and hear what happens in the rest of the Universe(U), see and hear what we can't see or hear.

This is how, for example, the earth would look from Jupiter, using a telescope:

(Maybe even smaller.)

Those women have found traces of calcium from the bones of their dead. Astronomers, on the other hand, measure the calcium in the stars. We (my Brother(B) and I) have other kinds of problems with calcium: empty milk cartons neither of us has drunk from, pieces of cheese that disappear from the refrigerator without having been tasted.

This is more or less how the stars look from Earth on a clear night:

The whole Universe(U), even time, is made up of the same material.

From a plane, a person would look smaller than this (or maybe not look like anything at all):

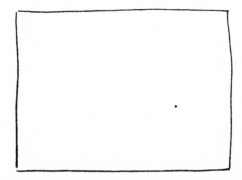

The body of her husband is there, or at least the remains of his calcium, and that woman knows it. But it's like knowing nothing, because the Atacama Desert is vast.

Several people would look smaller than this from a plane:

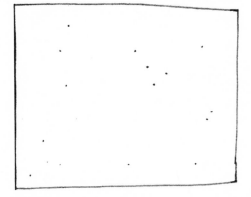

Astronomers don't know much either, that's why they build telescopes.

It's said every answer to a question is a new question. That too is something uniting us: neither astronomers, nor those searching for the disappeared, nor my Brother(B), nor I know anything. We're all trying to find traces, or asking ourselves questions.

We're all waiting for what we can't see to finally appear.

Translated by Christina MacSweeney • Spanish | Mexico

Here's where this story ends.

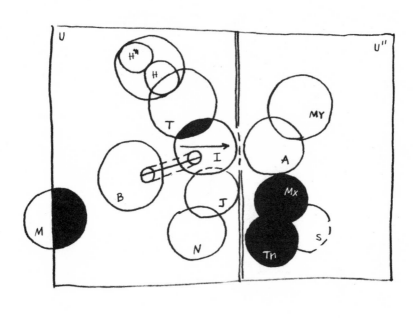

Translated by Christina MacSweeney • Spanish | Mexico

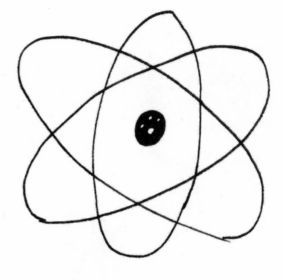

Typed *cone* into the library search engine the following day, and chose three texts: *Shadow Cone*, "Calculation of the Thickness of a Worm Gear Derived from the Cone," and "A Historical Reconstruction of the Quaternary Period in the Vegetation of the Southern Cone of America: An Interdisciplinary Approach." The poems in the first were an immediate disappointment. Closed my eyes, picked out a page at random, and ran my finger down to:

> *Place this line on the precise dot*
> *and we'll make love in Morse code.*

Laughed aloud and the book fell to the floor; a couple of people turned their heads, but no one seemed annoyed. The second text had diagrams and a lot of formulae; spent quite a while studying them, hoping to understand all those numbers, letters, brackets, and signs, but couldn't. Did manage to deduce that the "worm" of a gear refers to the serpentine engravings on the screw. In other words, it's what makes it different from a nail, and—not so sure about this—the cone is the head of the screw. In any case, there was no point in attempting to understand it all. The third text was from a journal of biology. There, for the first time, was a mention of my secret vocation: the keyword, *dendrochronology*. I smiled. No, that's not true. Went to look up *dendrochronology* in a dictionary, and that's when I smiled.

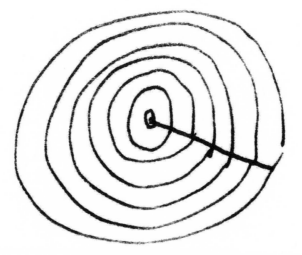

Translated by Christina MacSweeney • Spanish | Mexico

Based on that finding, it seemed a good idea to work in the Biology Institute Library. Guess Violeta and her boyfriend didn't quite understand how I ended up there, since my major had been visual arts, but they went along with it because, from their very personal point of view, the important thing was "supporting me." I didn't completely understand why I was there. What I wanted to research was the idea of time on the pine plywood boards; to find a way of understanding how it's transformed in the graining and conical sections. Dendrochronology was a means of studying time and space without going up in a rocket or solving quantum physics equations. Curiously enough, it was an astronomer who discovered the language of trees. Like me, Andrew Ellicott Douglass had strayed off the path. He was working on sunspots and ended by studying the rings in tree trunks to see if they could tell him anything about the sun. It's not only a matter of knowing the age of the trees: the history of the forests where they lived is recorded in the designs in the wood. The trees retain the scars of fires and every sort of natural disaster: earthquakes, hurricanes, diseases. Insects also leave their mark. You can even check the age of a violin or a piece of furniture by calculating the rings in the wood. A trunk is the compass of the ecosystem. And cutting down a forest isn't just an ecological tragedy; it is, quite literally, the destruction of an archive of historical data. But trees write in a language that can't be seen. Wonder what my life would look like inside a tree trunk, what all those lines, knots, and circumferences would mean.

Wonder how a set of truncated principles, an abrupt ending, or a disappearance would be written in that language.

KAMIL BOUŠKA is a contemporary Czech poet whose debut solo collection, *Oheň po slavnosti*, received two nominations for the Czech national Magnesia Litera award, in the Poetry and Discovery of the Year categories. His most recent collection of poetry is *Hemisféry*.

Sirény

Vítr mě ovinul jak prsten prst
   a byl to horký, režný stisk,
   zadřel se do hlasu a nesliboval dech.
Cizím jazykem tlačím ven chumel chlupů
   slepený slinami a krví,
bolestivý uzel drtí všechno, co je ze zpěvu—
   hladit jen proti srsti. Slova proti hlasu.
Vítr mě ovinul jak prsten prst
   a sirény houpou vzduchem.

Translated by
ONDREJ PAZDIREK

Sirens

The wind has coiled me the way a ring does a finger
    and it was a hot, rye grip
      that jammed into my voice, not promising breath.
With a foreign tongue I'm pushing out a tangle of hair
    glued together with saliva and blood,
a painful knot grinds all that is made of song—
    pet only against the grain. Words against voice.
The wind has coiled me the way a ring does a finger
    and sirens swing the air.

Translated by Ondrej Pazdirek • Czech | Czech Republic

Slavnost

Teď se ždímají šťávy v tělech
  a vzduch dusnější než některé rozkoše,
  lehává v našem smíchu.
Ozvěna hlasů velebí vtip,
  ten těžký kurevnický polibek,
  který si rozestlal v časech, kdy se nic neděje.
Sytí jak moře, čecháme žízeň s prosbou o vlnu, ale
  jako by klima zbarvilo vše nastejno, obcházíme stůl
  a jenom doléváme do prázdných sklenic.
Potichu otevírám svou hlavu a vyháním svět.

A Party

Now the bodily juices are wrung
   and the air, more stifling than some pleasures,
   lays down in our laughter.
The echo of voices extols wit,
   that heavy whoremonger kiss
   that unmakes its bed in times when nothing happens.
Satiated like the sea, we ruffle thirst in a plea for a wave, but
   as if the climate colored everything the same, we round the table
   and merely refill empty glasses.
Quietly, I'm opening my head and driving the world out.

Translated by Ondrej Pazdirek • Czech | Czech Republic

Konfese

Znovu se uzdravíš.
Město náhle rozechvělé
slunečným odpolednem, kypře přijímá
hojivou řeku světla z oblohy.
Obnažené, znovu ladí každý krok
a rozehrává jarní akord
na strunách ulic. Ve vzduchu vůně spí
jak smích ve tvém těle—
ozvěna příští, odpočaté melodie.
Slyším vlaky a v nich dálku. Psal jsem ti z vlaku
rukou, která jí nepatřila.
Silou jsem tiskl slova do papíru,
a přece jimi lomcoval průvan. Odkud?
Nevím, ale později nad postelí,
ve kterés mohla v tu chvíli ležet jen ty,
jako bych se dotýkal mlhy. Co jsem mohl?
Mohl jsem jen milovat všechny ty blízké obrysy,
které mlhou nebyly.
Teď se zdá, že skáčou přes laťku událostí,
aby slavnostním výrazem uhranuly paměť:
Šaty složené přes opěradlo,
jako by právě vydechly svůj objem,
zbytky vousů v umyvadle,
nehybnost se stopami chvatu.
Tanec zanícený nehybností.
Znovu se uzdravíš. Průhledné hlavy stromů
skoněné nad ulicí, tají šum ptačích křídel.
Sypký zvuk rezonuje večerem a vrší tenkou zář
na modrou hladinu.
Zpěv se za snem skryl, jen tvůj dech

Confession

You'll be well again.

The city, suddenly aquiver

with a sunny afternoon, aerates, accepting

the curative river of light from the sky.

Exposed, it once again tunes each step

and plucks a spring chord

on the strings of streets. In the air a fragrance sleeps

like laughter in your body—

the reverberation of a future, rested melody.

I hear trains and in them distance. I wrote to you from one,

using a hand that didn't belong to itself.

With force I pressed words into paper,

and still the draft rattled them. Where from?

I don't know, but later, above the bed

in which only you could have lain in that moment,

I felt as if I was touching fog. What could I?

I could only love all those near contours

that weren't fog.

Now it seems they leap over the bar of events

in order to bewitch memory with a festive expression:

A dress folded across the backrest,

as if it just exhaled its volume,

residue of a beard in the sink,

stillness with traces of haste.

A dance ingrown with stillness.

You'll be well again. The see-through heads of trees,

bent over the street, conceal the murmur of birds' wings.

A grainy sound resonates through the evening and heaps a thin glow

onto the blue surface.

The singing has hidden behind a dream, only your breath

Translated by Ondrej Pazdirek • Czech | Czech Republic

loví zlato ze dna.

Dívám se do vlhké tmy za oknem

a slyším tlumené hlasy. Před sebou

tvůj dopis, málem poslední.

Jiné písmo, jiná náplň, slova:

Stébla s horkou dužinou, oválná, pevná,

s rozbolavěnými konci stonků,

nelapají po vzduchu. Jsou z našeho těla,

ve kterém jsme tančili dokud nedozněl poslední

hlas. Znovu jej navíjím na cívku odpočatých tónů.

Znovu se uzdravíš. Čas není květem ze zánětu.

A láska nerostla ze sražené krve.

is fishing out gold from the bottom.
I'm looking into the damp darkness behind the window,
hearing subdued voices. In front of me
your letter, nearly last.
Different handwriting, different content, words:
Culms with hot pith, oval, firm,
with aching stem endings,
do not snatch at the air. They're from our body,
in which we danced until the last voice
died away. Once more I'm winding that voice up on the coil
  of rested tones.
You'll be well again. Time isn't a blossom from a wound.
And love didn't grow from clotted blood.

Translated by Ondrej Pazdirek • Czech | Czech Republic

ZSUZSA TAKÁCS, born in 1938, started publishing her work in the 1970s and is considered the doyenne of contemporary Hungarian poetry. Her spare and often intimately personal poetry and short prose addresses private and historical traumas, the impotence of language when faced with suffering. She lives in Budapest.

A test feltámadása

Állandóan az az érzés kísért, hogy igazi életem már elmúlt,
és amit életnek hiszek, halál utáni létezés csupán.
—John Keats levele Charles Brownnak

A villamosmegálló felé közeledve szabálytalanul és elszántan, átvágtam a síneken, mielőtt megindult volna a bevetésre kész autók rohama a gyalogosok ellen. Az egyik mellettem haladó a rajt pillanatában még cigarettára is gyújtott, hogy otthonosabban mozoghasson a kipufogógázok sűrű felhőjében. Az engedetlenség dúslombú erdeje suttogott fölöttem. A lombjairól visszaverődő fény bevilágította kamaszkorom ösvényeit és a diktatúrákban eltöltött későbbi évtizedeket. Súlyos koronája megóvott attól, hogy mindenestől elnyeljen az otthontalanság, amelynek neve: Budapest. Szememet a földre szögezve jártam az idő múltával egyre elhanyagoltabb utcákat, nehogy nyakamat szegjem a kukák körül rajzó hajléktalanok által szétdobált krumpli-, narancs- és banánhéjakon. Vigyázva keltem át a kutyaürülékkel sűrűn pettyezett járdákon, de az uszoda közelében, a Margit-kórház galambpiszok szegélyezte épülete előtt már elfogott a szabadulók mámora. Tudtam, hogy nemsokára úszószemüvegem zöld plexilapján keresztül nézhetem az égen vonuló felhőket.

Húsz éve is talán, egy barátom felajánlotta, beszél ismerősével, a piarista...

Zsuzsa Takács • The Resurrection of the Body

Translated by
ERIKA MIHÁLYCSA

The Resurrection of the Body

I have a habitual feeling of my real life having past,
and that I am leading a posthumous existence.
—John Keats to Charles Brown

Approaching the tram station I crossed the tracks, relentlessly jaywalking, before the cars ready for the sortie would have started their onslaught against the pedestrians. One of these walking by my side even lighted his cigarette at the moment they started up, to feel more at home in the heavy clouds of exhaust gas. Above me the thick foliage of the forest of disobedience was whispering. The light reflected on the foliage illuminated the paths of my puberty and the successive decades spent in dictatorships. Its massive crown saved me from being swallowed up entirely by the homelessness whose name is Budapest. With eyes fixed on the ground I walked the streets that ran ever more derelict with the passage of time, for fear I might break my neck on the potato, banana, and orange peels scattered by the bums swarming around the trash cans. With utmost care I crossed the sidewalk thickly dotted with dog poo, but near the swimming pool, in front of the block of Margit Hospital framed by pigeon droppings, I was seized by the exultation of those to be liberated. I knew that in a few minutes I would watch the clouds traveling across the sky through the green plexiglass of my swimming goggles.

Translated by Erika Mihálycsa • Hungarian | Hungary

It was about twenty years ago that a friend of mine offered to talk with an acquaintance of his, the reputed teacher of the Piarist college who was also an amateur psychologist, to help me dissipate my stalking depression. Besides his teaching duties—and without payment—this man would assist persons who found themselves in a difficult moment of their lives. For long, tedious one-and-half hours I would sit in his office, in the building where I used to be a boarding student in preparatory school. The place, the sight of the beggar squatting on the building's corner was oppressive. I was disheartened by the fact that during our conversations I had to tactfully avoid the problems related to my marriage, as the teacher was also a cleric. By spring I had had enough of our barren conversations, the filling in of innumerable test sheets, my improvised responses to the Rorschach blots. I was embarrassed by my weekly sneaking inside the ecclesiastical building, and I felt sore for wasting not only my but his time as well. So eventually I thanked him for his efforts, saying that by now I would surely manage on my own. For our last interview—as a farewell present—and half in jest, to alleviate my anxieties, he prepared my horoscope. It was thus armed with the promising constellation enclosed therein that I stepped out on the street—right into the arms of our institute's party secretary. I had to give her a detailed account of my doings inside the building. She rested her oil-green gaze gently on me all the time while I recounted that I was in the middle of a divorce and in need of psychological assistance. She told me that her own marriage was in crisis, so she could perfectly understand, and adding physical aid to her verbal consolations, she reached under my elbow, raising it as if she were leading me along a rough portion of the path. She proposed that from time-to-time we should meet and have a talk, so in the times to come I had to avoid not only the college building but the sympathetic proximity of the party secretary as well, and I would approach the Institute furtively, from the other end of the street. To do her justice though, whether offended or not, she didn't disclose our secret. But to come back to my horoscope compiled by the long dead teacher, I have to say it painted a luminous future for me.

His prophesy included a restrictive phrase though: namely, that the turn for the better would only occur toward the end of my life. I have never taken drugs, nor drunk seriously, unless I count the occasional flings during my trips. In the wainscoted restaurant of the chalet, the terminus of my tourist outings in the Pilis Mountains, in company or on my own, I always enjoyed putting down one or two glasses of rum, or a couple of jugs of beer. Yet my enlightenment, a few months ago, happened in the manner known from the accounts of addicts. On that memorable morning I was overcome by a violent sense of happiness. I tried to explain the change with my professional successes, eventually with the moving of our offices from the Józsefváros to the clean and tidy government district, but most likely it all boiled down to the fact that I had entered the last phase of my life.

I was waiting for the tram on the Buda bridgehead of Margit Bridge, there was no car traffic, the road, usually so overcrowded, was empty, when I suddenly caught a whiff of orange groves. My eyes fell on the orange-red parapet around the refuge island and my heart jumped, as I realized that the paint bore not only the color of oranges but their intensive scent as well. Enraptured, I stood there and looked around: does anybody else sense the inebriating perfume filling the air, but the others didn't appear to be sniffing at all, they stood about with serious faces. A man with a hat and, at his heels, a woman bowed under the weight of her shopping bags crossed the refuge island at a trot, giving no heed to the per-

My senses were celebrating the freshly discovered richness of the world.

fumed torrent, and nearly knocked me over. A warm autumn breeze blew from the Danube. It slightly lifted and dressed the blouse of a slender, tall, full-bosomed woman standing a few steps away from me, the two of them shared the undulation of the daisies painted on the silken fabric. I was moved by the woman's bold closeness, I had the feeling that she would gladly allow me to pick one or two flowers from her blouse. I had already let several trams pass by, passengers came and went, the wind blew snatches of conversation toward me, yet she stayed on, at times even glancing at me, she let me, suffered me look at her. When I had had my fill of the sight, I worked out the secret of her presence. All she wanted was to let me know that it was for my sake that the daisies of unsurpassable beauty were undulating on the silky meadow on her blouse, it was for my sake that the feeble autumn sun shone, that the paper bags of squash seeds were rustling, that the shoe heels were clicking in the tram stop, that the parapet was pouring forth its inebriating scent. Once I had grasped this I thanked heaven and got on tram

Translated by Erika Mihálycsa • Hungarian | Hungary

number four. I could see the woman starting from the tram stop toward the underground passage. I was not overcome by the usual melancholia that I wouldn't see her again. It was I who had decided, I thought, that I would rest in the world and own its riches for a while only. Calm descended on me. I didn't care that the girl in sneakers threw the rich apple-core remains of her snack under the seat. My eyes were not upset by the bundle-dragging migration, easy to trace from the window, of the scavengers, or by the opalescent glinting of the aluminum booth in front of the Franciscan church. My senses were celebrating the freshly discovered richness of the world.

"Has something happened?" my colleagues asked. "Why are you so happy?" "Something happened," I answered mysteriously. Everybody thought of women, or of one particular woman, although this time it was something completely different. Now I was certain that my waiting in a dusty corner of the world had come to an end, my suitcase stood packed in the antechamber, the day of my journey was settled. I took leave of everybody and everything at length. I meticulously observed every place where I settled for half an hour, or for a whole morning for a department meeting. I took my pencil in my palm, longing to feel its butterfly weight; I smoothed over the drawing sheet, the grooves of my compass, my ruler; I followed, engrossed, the seam's up-and-downward slides on our young secretary's waist, the movement of strangers on the street, the gentle descent of leaves on the surface of puddles, the cascade of sparks of the tram's current collector. My eyes absorbed all sights. As though I had to memorize every detail in order to be able to report later to someone what my earthly life had been like, what the odor of spices was like, the cut of coats, the meandering itinerary of raindrops on the pavement, the girls' laughter. Before sleeping in I would list the wondrous events of the day, so that I might dream them again. I got emotional when touching the door handle, I gave a manly grip to the hand held out to me. In the bliss of enhanced perception I listened with closed eyes to the rippling of sounds around me. I waited for vehicles in a state of felicity.

For months rapture persisted; as if every step of mine had been blessed and guided by a protective glance, I walked the edge of the precipice of every day blindly, but perfectly safe. Then on an October day, as though a pebble got into my shoe or a grit of sand into my eye, ill humor swept over me, my lust for life started ebbing. I was sitting in dark rooms again at home or at the office. I stood stiff, tense at the reception desk, tormented by the memory of what I had failed to do. A verse stuck in my mind: "Stand slow, little heart, in the staircase," and as if at a summons, the figure of my sister, nine years younger than me, who later settled in Switzerland and died there, emerged from willing oblivion. After the death of our parents she lived with me for a while in our old home, and in the first years of my independence the responsibility of her upbringing felt like a hunch on my back. I didn't care much about the fact that she had no key to our shared apartment, or more precisely, I arranged things in such a way that she had no key and so could not break in on me at an unexpected moment. Indeed it happened on more than one occasion that I arrived home late and found her lingering in the staircase, or asleep with her back to the wall on our doormat, wrapped up in her coat, locked out from our home, with foggy eyes and arms embracing her spread-out hair. This memory now found me, it haunted me even in sleep. I am sleeping in my bed when I notice that she is waiting in front of our door to be let in, although she too is inside, in the room.

I am deluding and sedating myself again, my imagined suitcase has disappeared from the antechamber, the date of my journey has been postponed...

I want to touch her reddish-blond, as they say, unruly tresses, but she draws away from my caress, it seems she hasn't forgotten, in vain I go to pains to explain. What is awful is that at the time she didn't object to anything, and now I can't repair what happened. She died in a car accident, just like our parents. But whereas they plunged into the precipice on the Niš highway in Yugoslavia when they surfaced from a dark tunnel into the dazzling light of the serpentines, she crashed into a rock wall on an empty road, in excellent visibility, bouncing into the ravine between Kulm and Vitznau.

So the strict daily schedule was reinstalled: office, swimming pool, sleeping pills. The treadmill routine. I am deluding and sedating myself again, my imagined suitcase has disappeared from the antechamber, the date of my journey has been postponed, my razor, toothbrush, and hair lotion have been placed back on the smeared glass shelf. On the street leading to the tram station I jaywalk across the tracks before the cars ready for the sortie start their onslaught against the pedestrians. A fellow jaywalker even lights

Translated by Erika Mihálycsa • Hungarian | Hungary

a cigarette. I am coming from the swimming pool, my throat is a bit sore, there is a suspect, vagrant warmth around my pulse, the herald of the usual strep throat. A driver with an enormous copper ring in one ear gives voice to his indignation over my forbidden crossing with a long honk. He doesn't slow down, it seems he wants to teach me a lesson. The others brake, as though resignedly accepting the fact that the pedestrians, condemned to an overlong crossing in the deathly air, ignore the road markings. But my man with the copper earring doesn't give up, he draws a narrow circle around me, braking and honking deafeningly.

If I didn't know that he has been dead for two years, I would think P. is coming toward me, arm in arm with his wife. Around the woman's neck a scarf tied in a minxish knot above a worn sweater, with the intellectual woman's maladroit heedlessness of both danger and style. Seriousness permeates their figures. I buy a paper, pick a relatively dirt-free portion of the stone parapet around the subway entrance where I could rest my heavy shoulder bag and sit down. They appear again. What a prodigious, self-destructive architect he was! Who did I hear the incredible news of his death from, or who am I mixing him up with? I peer out at them from behind my paper; there is something unusual in his face. Could this smooth-faced double be his younger brother? Yet it is curious that he should be emulating P.'s dressing style and team up with his wife. He is wearing a dark blue jacket and gray trousers with a knife-edge crease. Could he have inherited P.'s wardrobe? I couldn't say that the fate of the personal possessions of the dead distresses or saddens me. While I am musing, I can see that they have come close. I stand up, call his name, but my hand held out rests in the air. He doesn't answer, doesn't halt, we don't pat each other on the shoulder. If I wanted, I could stick my fingers right through him, as if his body presented no obstacle to my fingers. In the end he takes his wife's arm and they turn to leave in the direction of Széna Square, where my episode with the earringed driver played out a short while ago, and where an accident investigation is in course.

In a pleasant torpor I am waiting for tram fifty-nine to pull in the station. A new vehicle arrives, the seats are still covered in nylon overlay, the metal poles are flashing impeccably, the leather grab handles are aligned. It is true that the request stop buttons are not working yet, the passengers need to get used to the new technique first, that one day the doors, which still open automatically, would only open on demand. They make sure that it would not affect us adversely, that we should make up our minds whether to get off or travel on. Still, there is no malice in me, it is merely my phrasing that is perhaps too trenchant. I enjoy lingering in the spacious, illuminated interior, the stops rush by, the doors open up readily: Open Sesame! I recall with nostalgia my spacious home among the fir trees, the fence with the walnut branches leaning over from the neighboring garden. In front of my eyes the sharp crease of P.'s trousers appears suddenly, and his blazing striped shirt that he had coveted so much. I open the mailbox: a bunch of death notices fall into my hand.

Translated by Erika Mihálycsa • Hungarian | Hungary

FRIEDERIKE MAYRÖCKER's most
recent volume of poetry is *Scardanelli*,
an invocation of the late nineteenth-century
poet Friedrich Hölderlin. Mayröcker
writes in the hallucinatory register she
herself has often identified as post-surreal
while simultaneously professing an acutely
personal voice and vision.

ich öffne weinend die Tür und es fällt mir vor die Füsze : fällt

mir ein DIE DEMUTH und an der Türschwelle *das nackte Gewässer*

Höld. Hungerblümchen mein Herz gebückt : pochend mit den lauen

Regengüssen wie einst in D., *bleich* bin ich geworden und immer noch

voll Sehnsucht, während der *bleiche* Himmel am Fenster, demütig

unterwürfig sogar kein Quentchen Stolz in mir, da ich müszig und

still über die Berge wo die trinkbaren Frühlingsblüthen, oder

mit Tränen den Tag (anhebt der Tag der Morgen dessen wilde

Seele) eingeschlossen in mein Gelasz während drauszen der Frühling

mit seinen mächtig sprieszenden Kelchen *weil es listet die Seele*

Höld. während in den Armen der Mutter : der Vögel welche vorüber-

brausen an meinem Fenster: ahne nur ihre Natur, in den Auen die

weiszen Matten von tausenden Schneeglöckchen weisze Schneeglöck-

chen Felder in den Auen (*solche Fäustlinge* : 1 Verlesung) des

Wiener Waldes nämlich die Begängnisse der weiszen Blumen

2-flügelig deine schwarze Hand wie du an der Tür des "K1. Café"

Franziskanerplatz vorüber im Dämmerschein (schwarzer Mantel),

ich fahre durch 1 Postkarte begabte Bäume (diese Süszigkeit : *latin*

lover smarter Kellner im Cafe Tirolerhof mit Affektion und ent-

zündender Jüngling mit schwarzer Locke / *das Nerven und Tanzen*)

ahnungslos bin ich die Ovarien schlafen, sagt Edith S., bin see-

lenkrank hl.Onanie bin ahnungslos auf der *Wiese verweilen die Schaafe*

ahnungslos bin ich rapide wechselt die Natur ihre ZEILEN = Zeiten

Translated by
JONATHAN LARSON

I open the door crying and it falls at my feet : it comes to
me THE HUMILITY and at the threshold *the naked waters*
Höld. shadflower my heart hunched over : thumping with the tepid
downpours as once in D., I turned *pale*
and still full of longing, while the *pale* sky at the window, humbly
submissive not even 1 grainlet of pride in me, as I'm idle and
quiet over the mountains where the drinkable springblossomes, or
with tears the day (lifts up the day the morning whose wild
soul) enclosed in my room while outside the spring
with its mighty sprouting goblets *as it lists the soul*
Höld. while in the arms of the mother : the birds which breeze
on past my window : only intimate at their nature, in the isles the
white mats of thousands of snowdrops white snow-
drops fields in the isles (*such fistlings* : 1 misreading) of the
vienna woods namely the *obits* of the white flowers
2-winged your black hand as you at the door of the "little café"
past the Franziskanerplatz in the gloaming dawn (black coat), I
drive through 1 postcard gifted trees (this sweetness : *latin
lover* smart waiter in the Café Tirolerhof with affection and en-
flaming youth with black curl / *the nerving and dancing*)
I'm all unawares the ovaries are sleeping, says Edith S., am soul-
sick holy onanism am all unawares on the meadow *the sheepe whiling*
am all unawares *rapidly* nature switches its LINES = times

sie ist auszer sich auszer Atem, kann zusehen wie sie aus Schnee-
flocken Feldlerchen macht aus Eisblumen junge Blättchen, dieses
zerzauste Flüstern der 1. Tulpenkelche

in tiefer Nacht die Nähe deiner Stimme in tiefer Nacht die Trauer
deines Herzens sehe die zärtlichen Veilchen in deinen Augen, so
faszt du mich an der Hand während wie 1 Lauffeuer Kandinskys "exo-
tische Vögel" von 1915. Die entzündete Brust der Strophen an die
Hügel gelehnt *während grüner lebendiger Epheu*

29.2.08

beside itself out of breath, can see how it makes sky-
larks from snowflakes young leaflets out of frost-flowers, this
tousled whispering of the 1st tulip-goblets
in deep night the nearness of your voice in deep night the sorrow
of your heart I see the tender violas in your eyes, thus
you grasp me by the hand while like 1 wildfire Kandinsky's "exo-
tic birds" from 1915. The enflamed breast of the verses leaned
against the hills *while green living ivy*

2/29/08

Translated by Jonathan Larson • German | Austria

An.

dasz ich so unterthan bin wohl geh ich täglich zum
Felsen, wo die Rosen, blühn (Hold.), dieser Blick
vom Bang groszen grünen Hang hinab in die *murmelnde* Stadt
Florenz damals so stand ich stand auf dem grünen
Hügel der voll Ölbäumen oder ich blickte vom Fenster
aus in den Hain der Ölbäume (Hain) dasz mir zitterte das
Herz ich war noch in meiner Jugend und der Himmel unendlich
schien über der Stadt Florenz damals mit Sara, Roberto, an
SEINER Hand, lang standen wir so, versunken in den Anblick der
(*inszenierten*) Stadt Florenz wahrend die vielen Jahre der
Liche noch vor mir Jahre der Trauer der Ttanen der Sehnsucht
unwissend ahnungslos ich (*wenn ich wie 1 unzeitige Blüthe*) Hold.
wohl geh ich oftmals in deinem Schatten in deiner Weis-
heit seh bald ins Grüne der Fluren des Wiener Walds aber nimmer
vergesz ich den Blick von der Anhöhe (waren die Graser schon
gelb?) in die liebliche Stadt Florenz, mit den Freunden.
Gealtert nun nach so vielen Frühlingen Wintern flüchtigen
Sommern, belauscht im Laube damals mein Herz
(wahrend am Horizont der Saum der atemlosen Zypressen)

für Kurt Neumann

4.3.08, 5 Uhr früh

To.

that I'm so subservient surely I'll go daily to the
rock wall, where the roses bloome (Höld), this lookout
from the cliff down the great green cliff into the *murmuring* city
Florence that time and so I stood on the green
hill full of olive trees or I looked from the window
out into the grove of olive trees (grove) that trembled in me the
heart I was still in my youth and the sky endlessly
seeming over the city Florence then with Sara, Roberto, with
HIS hand, we stood like that for a long time, sunken in the sight of the
(*staged*) city of Florence while the many years of
love still before me years of sorrow of tears of longing
unknowing unawares I (*when I as 1 untimely blossome*) Höld.
surely I'll often go in your shadow in your wis-
dom seeing into the green of the floors of the vienna woods soon
but nevermore forgetting the view from the height (were the grasses
already yellow?) onto the lovely city Florence, with friends.
Aged now after so many springs winters fleeting
summers, my heart eavesdropped in the foliage that time
(while on the horizon the seam of the breathless cypress)

for Kurt Neumann

3/4/08—5:00 in the morning

Translated by Jonathan Larson • German | Austria

der lächelnde weisze Schwan auf dem weißen Badetuch = Scardanelli Version

da ich/ wie junge Füchse stanken (geographischen Eltern) da ich
1 Knabe war, Hölderlin, Rose von Schnee inmitten Frühling, endlich
im Gehäuse Maria Callas' Stimme Vogel Musik erlesene stürmende
stürzende Träne in Erinnerung jenes Sommers in Altaussee : Was-
sermannhaus mit Hans H. und Helene als wir auf dem schmalen Bal-
kon und in der Tiefe der See schwärmte im Dämmerschein des

                                    .   Abends

und *geselligen Bäume* -   und scheu der Vogel der Nacht trauert
wie einst Thomas Kling auf der geborstenen Säule mit ausgebreiteten Flügeln
ehe er starb dieser rauhe und zärtliche Held : Liebling
des Gesanges sein Aventüre Leben nämlich *schlenkerte* mit den
Armen/ *overdressed die Natur* indessen unbeweint werde ICH sein
o du prophetische
die verblühten Mimosen in der zerscherbten Vase die ehmals blühen-
den duftenden Sträusze : Süsze der Bäume : nun nur noch Gespenst
Gestrüpp Skelett (wie auch wir dereinst usw.) und ahmt die kl.Schrit-
te die immer wehrloseren Schritte des Leibs der Seele / und immer

the smiling white swan on the white beach towel = Scardanelli Version

as I / stunk like young foxes (geographical parents) as I
was 1 young boy, Hölderlin, snow rose in the midst of spring, finally
in the housing Maria Callas' voice bird music exquisitely read storming
startling in plunging tear in memory of that summer in Altausee : Was-
sermannhaus with Hans H. and Helene as we on the skinny bal-
cony and in the deep the lake swarmed in the gloaming dawn of the evening
and communing trees -   and shyly the bird of the night mourns
as once Thomas Kling on the burst pillar with outspread
wings before he died this raw and tender hero : darling
of song his adventure life namely *swerved* with
arms / *overdressed nature* in the meantime unlamented will I be
o you prophetic
the faded mimosas in the shattered vase the formerly blossome-
ing scenting bouquets : sweetness of the trees : now only the ghost
undergrowth skeleton (as we also once on 1 time etc.) and itates the little strides
the evermore defenseless strides of the body of the soule / and ever
(*nevermore*) have I lifelong concealed the pain the panic the

Translated by Jonathan Larson • German | Austria

(*nimmer*) habe verborgen ich lebenslang den Schmerz die Panik die
Einsamkeit, in meinen geflügelten Wohnungen, habe auf 1 x die rote
Lilie gesehen auf dem Parkett im roten Patio (*Pomp*) Durch die
jungen Blättchen hindurch kann ich ihn sehen und als dunkle Vogel-
schwinge an meinem Auge vorüber vermutlich Strähne aus meinem

Haar

am Morgen in der Waldtiefe im Windbruch nämlich seitlicher Blick
aus halb verhangenem Himmel sah ich ihn vorüber *weiden und wischen*
zu (Garten) Garben die geselligen Bäume Höld., im rauhen Frühlinge
wo die Weinberge und geplätteten Felder da oben beim Wegkreuz wo
wir wandelten/ stillestanden, schauten den weiszen Horizont der sich
entzündet hatte in weiszer Glut (glimmt und schimmert und *schädel-
frei*) nämlich Leberblümchen WILD am Waldrand, und wie der Boden
blau sich verfärbte

24.3.08

loneliness, in my winged apartments, have looked all at once on the red

Lily on the parquet on the red patio (*pomp*). On through the

young leaflets I can see him and as dark bird-

pinions past my eyes presumably 1 strand of my hair

in the morning in the deep of the woods in the windfall namely side

    glance

from half overcast sky I saw him *grazing and browsing* over past

to (garden) garb the communing trees Höld., in the raw springs

where the vineyards and iron pressed fields up there by the wayside cross

    where

we walked and wended / stood still, looking at the white horizon that had

enflamed itself in white glow (gleams and shimmers and *skull-*

free) namely liverwort WILD at the woods' edge, and how the ground

turned itself blue

3/24/08

Translated by Jonathan Larson • German | Austria

dann hört alles plötzlich auf auch die Lerche Narzisse die
Nachtigall die unscheinbar in dem Blätterdach die ich nie sah
nie hörte, die mit roten offenen Schnäbeln pfeilenden Dorfschwal-
ben : die sind jetzt 80 die werden lange leben auch die rosa
Päonien in den fremden Gärten, die Zeisige Wühlmäuse Maulwür-
fe die in den Grabhügeln wohnen. Dann geht mir die Sprache verloren : abhanden, der Mond dem sie lange schon sein Geheimnis
entwunden, die 1 .Kirschen, die Gänseblümchen der Mohn, die kl.
Hunde, Weiszdorn, und Nachtviolen, *die Bürde meines Gewissens* das
Kästchen mit der Asche der letzten Verwandten alles verloren her-
ausgerissen aus meinem Herzen getilgt keine Erinnerungen mehr an
die Erde : Glorie Welt
(fand heute morgen den Regenschirm des Freundes gänzlich verstaubt
und verbogen in diesen 8 Jahren da man vergessen auf ihn...)
"love me love my umbrella," James Joyce

behutsam mit den Augen zu winken (mir nach) und liebkosen und
küssen mein letztes Gedicht : das eben fertig geschriebene aller-
letzte Gedicht und wie die Tränen drüberrollen dasz die Zeilen
zerflieszen nämlich 1 *Zirpen* das keiner mehr hört usw

5.19.08

then suddenly everything stops the lark daffodil the
nightingale that unapparent in the leafy canopy that I never saw
never heard, who with red open beaks arrowing village-swall-
ows : they're 80 now they'll live long the rosy
peonies also in the stranger gardens, the siskins root voles common
moles that live in the grave-mounds. Then the language is lost on me :
gone missing, the moon from which its long since
wrested its secret, the 1st cherries, the daisies, the poppies, the little
dogs, hawthorns, and night violas, *the burden of my conscience* the
boxlet with the ash of the last relations all is lost torn
from my heart deleted no more memories of
earth : glory world
(found the friend's umbrella this morning entirely covered in dust
and bent out of shape in these 8 years since 1's forgotten it...)
"love me love my umbrella," James Joyce

cautious to wink with the eyes (at me) and caress and
kiss my last poem : the just written and completed very
last poem and as the tears roll over it that the lines
dissolve namely 1 *chirping* that no 1 else ever hears etc

5/19/08

Translated by Jonathan Larson • German | Austria

YAN GE was born in Sichuan, China, and currently lives in Dublin. She is the author of eleven books and was chosen as Best New Writer by the Chinese Literature Media Prize. *People's Literature* magazine recently named her as one of China's twenty future literary masters.

悲伤兽

悲伤兽居住在永安城东北。锦绣河穿越城市中心，往东流，在洛定洲分为芙蓉河与孔雀河——悲伤兽居住在孔雀河南岸的那片小区。

小区很老了，墙壁爬满了壁虎，唤做乐业小区。原来是平乐纺织厂的职工宿舍，悲伤兽大半都是这个纺织厂的工人，很多年前，从南边来到永安城，住了下来。

悲伤兽性温和，喜阴冷。爱吃花菜和绿豆。香草冰淇淋和橙子布丁。惧火车，苦瓜及卫星电视。

雄悲伤兽长得高大，嘴巴大，手掌小，左小腿内侧有鳞片，右耳内侧有鳍。肚脐周围的皮肤为青色，除此以外，和常人无异。

雌悲伤兽面容美丽，眼睛细长，耳朵较常人大，身形纤弱，肤偏红，月满时三天不通人语，只做雀鸟之鸣，此外，与常人无异。

悲伤兽不笑，但笑即不止，长笑至死方休，故名悲伤。

悲伤兽的祖先，追溯上去，可能是上古时候的某个诗人，但年代久远，不可考证。

雄悲伤兽善手工，因此做纺织，雌兽貌美，因此多为纺织店售货...

Translated by
JEREMY TIANG

Sorrowful Beasts

The sorrowful beasts lived in the northeastern quarter of Yong'an City. As the Splendid River passed through the city center and headed east, it separated into the Lotus and Peacock Rivers in Luoding District. The beasts lived in a housing development on the Peacock's southern bank.

These old buildings, their walls thick with ivy, were known as the Leye Estate. They'd originally been built as dorms for the Pingle Cotton Mill, where many of the sorrowful beasts had worked for years, ever since they first came to Yong'an City from the south and settled here.

Sorrowful beasts were gentle by nature, and preferred the cold. They loved cauliflower and mung beans, vanilla ice cream and tangerine pudding. They feared trains, bitter gourd, and satellite television.

The males of the species were tall, with large mouths and small hands, scales on the insides of their left calves and fins next to their right ears. The skin around their belly buttons was dark green, but other than that, they were just like regular people.

Translated by Jeremy Tiang • Chinese | China

The females were beautiful—long, narrow eyes, ears a little larger than normal, delicate figures with reddish skin. For three days at the full moon, they lost the ability of human speech, squawking like birds instead. Otherwise, they were just like regular people.

> *Legend had it that a sorrowful beast's smile was so beautiful, no one who'd seen it could ever forget. But no matter how many jokes you told them, they never smiled.*

Sorrowful beasts never smiled. If they did, they wouldn't be able to stop, not until they died. Hence their name.

If you looked back far enough, you might trace their forebears to a poet from ancient times, too far back for there to be any evidence.

Male sorrowful beasts were skilled with their hands, which is how they ended up weaving textiles. The females, being good-looking, often worked as salesgirls in the fabric stores. The people of Yong'an City came shopping for cloth all the way across town, to this dilapidated little corner, all to catch a glimpse of these attractive beasts.

Legend had it that a sorrowful beast's smile was so beautiful, no one who'd seen it could ever forget. But no matter how many jokes you told them, they never smiled.

This made the loveliness of the female beasts seem all the more to be cherished and pitied, which caused the tycoons of Yong'an City to take pride in marrying them—the females could mate with humans, giving birth to children exactly the same as normal people. The males weren't able to do this, and so Leye Estate was filled with bachelors, while the ladies ended up in the wealthy district to the south, their faces like ice, fleeing so fast their feet barely touched the ground, leaving the estate increasingly desolate.

Zoologists raised an outcry in the newspapers: if things went on like this, these rare creatures would surely go extinct. The government passed a law that sorrowful beasts could only marry among their own kind, requiring special permission if they wished to couple with humans, to be decided by a tender every five years. This way, a beast-wife became an even greater mark of status, which the upper crust went mad for, while the government picked up a fair bit of revenue.

Lefty, a painter, was the friend of a friend. The stories about her and the sorrowful beast had spread far and wide among our circles, but few people knew the truth. One day, she came up to me at a party and said, I know you, you specialize in beastly tales. I want to tell you a sorrowful beast's story. Are you interested?

I said, Yes, but I have to pay you something.

Lefty said, I don't want anything at all.

But, I said, that's the rule, I have to give you something—I smiled, but her face remained blank.

She said, I'd love a vanilla ice cream.

I bought her one, and she devoured it with gusto, almost forgetting to speak.

I'd smoked two cigarettes before she finally opened her mouth again.

She said, My sorrowful beast died last week.

Lefty met the male beast at a time when the Pingle Mill was doing badly—all the salesgirls had run off to marry moneybags, leaving no one to sell the goods, so many workers got laid off. She first encountered him at the Dolphin Bar—he walked over and said to her, I've just lost my job, could you buy me a drink?

She looked up at him. He was very tall, with a serious expression, the skin of his face shiny and unwrinkled. All right, she said. As they drank, Lefty noticed an exquisite fin behind his ear. She said, You're a beast. He answered, Yes, and I'm out of work.

That night, he followed her home, and she tamed him.

The beast was named Cloud. He slept quietly at night, didn't talk much, loved baths, and ate nothing but three vanilla ice creams a day. If anyone turned on the TV, he'd let out a shattering howl and his eyes would flash red—his beastly nature revealing itself.

Lefty stopped watching television. When she got home, they'd sit at either end of the sofa, each reading a book. When he was happy, he'd let out a long cat-like rumble, but never smiled.

Translated by Jeremy Tiang • Chinese | China

At night they slept together, Cloud in the nude. His physique was just like a human male's. The skin around his belly button was green as the sea, even a little translucent. Lefty often found herself mesmerized by that patch of skin. It's so beautiful, she'd say.

She stroked him, and he purred like a contented cat, but they couldn't make love. It's because you're human, he explained.

They slept in each other's arms, like a couple of beasts.

It was a lovely time. The male beast was even more nurturing and good with his hands than a human girl—he cooked for Lefty and washed her clothes. The food was mostly vegetarian, and the laundry had a strange fragrance. As Lefty ate, he'd watch from across the table, his expression tender. She almost started to regard him as her husband.

This all happened last May. Lefty painted quite a few portraits, using the male beast as her model, and gave a very successful exhibition at Evergreen Gallery. Everyone knew she had a sorrowful beast with long, sturdy legs, a flat, greenish stomach, and bright, empty eyes. Standing or sitting, he became an object of affection for all the young women in the city.

●

I saw that exhibition. The first time I heard the rumors about Lefty and the sorrowful beast, our gossip king Little Worm said, That wench Lefty definitely slept with him. I said, Male beasts can't do it with humans. Little Worm sniggered, You believe that?

Yet I did believe this was a pure beast. In one of the paintings, he sat on a window sill, not a stitch on him, clearly showing the scales on his calf, his expression a little shy, and therefore captivating. Everyone thought how good-looking he'd be, if he would only smile.

But he didn't.

If he smiled, he would die.

He's dead, said Lefty now. She sat across from me, taking great mouthfuls out of her ice cream. She looked terrible, not smiling either.

●

Lefty said that on a full-moon night, they heard a long cry, like a phoenix. Cloud's eyes opened wide. Looking flustered, he ran to open the door— there was a girl standing outside. Even in the murky light of the corridor, you could see she was gorgeous. She couldn't speak, just let out another cry, then hugged him tightly.

Lefty asked her to come in and gave her a vanilla ice cream. The girl's skin was flushed red, as if blood was about to seep from it. Cloud said, She's sick.

This female beast was married to a rich man from the southern district. Cloud said she was his sister, named Rain. She relied on him, not leaving his side even when they slept. They got her to drink a tincture of woad, and still she wouldn't stop shrilling. Cloud didn't know what to do, so he called the human man, only to have him snap in frustration, She keeps screeching, and I don't know what she wants—after all, I'm not a beast!

Cloud hung up and hugged his sister, kissing her cheeks over and over again. Both beasts were now letting out similar cries. Sitting opposite them on the sofa, Lefty phoned her ex-boyfriend, Dr. Fu.

The doctor hurried over, looking—according to Lefty—even more hand- some than before. He nimbly took Rain's temperature and blood pressure, then gave her an injection. He said, She's pregnant, she needs this shot.

Lefty called Rain's husband, who was so overjoyed he could barely speak, practically in tears, thanking the heavens that the Wang family now had an heir! Lefty hung up in a rage. Next thing she knew, a Mercedes Benz was pulling up outside. When they said goodbye to Rain, she was still shrieking nonstop, though her body had grown less red.

Cloud was all sweaty, and went to take a shower. Dr. Fu paced around the living room, then suddenly embraced the painter and said, I've missed you.

They clung together, reminiscing about bygone days, touching and kiss- ing each other, their breath urgent. As they tangled, the splashing noises from the bathroom were like the warm embrace of ocean waves.

The next morning, Cloud was dead.

Lefty said, he never smiled, I don't know how he died.

I said, I don't know either.

The artist looked distraught, which made her even more beautiful. She said, I want to know how he died, I was practically in love with him.

The party that night ended abruptly, and I walked home. At the club entrance, I saw Lefty and a man whiz by in an expensive sports car, letting out a sharp cry.

The man next to me couldn't stop praising her. That chick, he said, Ever since she got herself a sorrowful beast, she's been reborn, her paintings are more stunning than ever, and so is she—wonder when I'll find one for myself.

He turned to me. Don't you know about these things? Go find me one.

I said, It takes destiny for a human to tame a beast.

He disagreed. How many beasts are there in Yong'an City? In the end, who knows who's taming whom.

I laughed, If you're scared, you should leave.

He said, No one who comes here is able to leave, this town is too full of monsters, too enchanting, too bewitching. A paradise for artists and wanderers.

I thought about the painter Lefty. I'd heard stories about her, many years ago, when she was new in town. She'd arrived here from the north, as coarse as gravel with her country accent. People laughed at her behind her back. And now, she'd become an elegant urban lady, her lips the color of blood, as if she'd been in this city all her life.

●

The sorrowful beasts came to the city many years ago and never left, never mind the dire warnings of zoologists, never mind floods or droughts or recessions or wars or stock-market crashes or epidemics, they just stayed put in Yong'an, their numbers stable, like an eternal riddle.

Fifty or sixty years ago, Yong'an had many types of beasts, and human beings were just one variety, but then war broke out, and then unrest, people doing battle against the beasts for a whole decade. This period of history had vanished, though it wasn't that long ago, but everyone only knew or pretended to only know the barest facts about it. Most of the beasts vanished, driven to extinction. The sorrowful beasts survived, and became the most dominant tribe in Yong'an City.

But no human being had truly gotten to know them. The females married out, but the males couldn't be with people.

And so, when I went online to search for information about sorrowful beasts, trying to find out how Cloud died, I found no leads apart from these scraps.

Maybe he ate too much bitter gourd and it killed him, I chuckled.

I phoned my university tutor, a famous Yong'an zoologist. I said, Have you researched sorrowful beasts? I need to know what could suddenly kill them, apart from smiling.

He was silent for a while, then said, Meet me for coffee tomorrow, we'll talk more then.

In the morning paper, I read about Lefty in the entertainment section—a story about her being spotted on numerous dates with the son of a famous construction magnate. In the accompanying picture, they were drinking at a rooftop bar, the man young and dashing, grinning smugly. You could make out Lefty's left profile, an eye-catchingly large loop dangling from one ear, her features exquisite, but calm and melancholy, unsmiling.

I took a sip of tea, and then another, and wondered if she was still in love with the dead beast.

The phone rang just then. It was my tutor again, saying, Have you seen today's paper? The picture of that lady painter.

I said I'd seen it. That's what I wanted to ask you about—it was her sorrowful beast who died.

A long silence, then he said, Listen to me, it's best if you don't go poking into this.

Why? I asked. Do you know how that beast died?

He may not have died, he said, and paused, His soul might be immortal.

I laughed, You're talking about the City of Souls?

This was a place that, according to legend, lay beneath Yong'an City, with humans and beasts, cars and roads, bands and their followers, all living forever. Every mother scared her child with this horror story: Don't sit too long on the toilet reading, because while you're distracted, a soul might rise up from the ground, through the toilet, and up into your body to take you

Translated by Jeremy Tiang • Chinese | China

over. This gave every kid a healthy respect for the toilet bowl, and it was only when they grew up that they realized they'd been tricked.

The phone was buzzing, the signal weak. He said, Anyway...what I meant was...

We got cut off.

When I was still a little girl, I used to squat by the toilet for a long time, staring and hoping a soul would float up to talk with me, never mind if it was human or beast. If one showed up, I'd say hello. That's the sort of courteous child I was. It was sure to like me.

●

I visited the female beast Rain in the wealthy district to the south. Her belly was already faintly swelling. She greeted me politely in the hall, saying, I've read your novels, they're very good.

She was drinking iced chocolate, and her skin glowed pearly pink, her voice soft and warm. She sat in a corner of the room, her back to the light, her eyes gleaming black.

A sense of unease prickled me as I said, I'm here to ask about your brother.

Rain's face was blank. She said, Brother? I don't have a brother.

As I gaped at her, the security guard briskly walked in from the outer chamber and said, Madam isn't feeling well, Miss, you should come again another day.

He was very tall and expressionless, the spitting image of a sorrowful beast, but he was human. His hands were big and strong—grabbing my arm, he said, This way, miss.

Rain remained on the sofa, guilelessly watching me. She said, What's wrong? Her ears were a little larger than normal, like a temple Buddha floating among the clouds, unaware of worldly torments, asking his acolytes, If they're hungry, why not just have a meat bun?

That night, at the Dolphin Bar, I ran into Little Worm with his new girlfriend, a cautious-looking lady who sipped a glass of orange juice as she sat silently next to us.

I bummed a cigarette off him, and told him what happened that morning. It's infuriating, I said, getting bullied like that.

I blew smoke right at his face, and he frowned as he waved it away. He said, It's not like you're new to this, didn't you know this would happen? You can't blame anybody else.

●

Our local government was on the People's Road, a cluster of unappealing squat gray buildings, with guards standing ramrod straight at the front entrances. Too many to take in at a single glance. God knows how many documents they pumped out into the world each day, to be passed around and recited, or peeped at.

Among these were the regulations for marriage between sorrowful beasts and humans: beforehand, the female beast should undergo hypnosis or surgery to eliminate her own beastly memory, and go for monthly hormone shots to suppress her beastly nature, which meant all beasts with human husbands had amnesia, forgetting who they were, or even that they were beasts. Sitting in their sumptuous living rooms, waiting for their husbands to come home, then disrobing and getting into bed with them, perpetuating the human race. Yet around the middle of each lunar month, when the moon was full, they'd recover their beastliness, losing the power of human speech. Afterward, they forgot what happened in those two or three days.

A new type of hormone was being invented that would leave the beasts unable to remember anything of their origins, even when the moon was at its roundest, instead remaining human forever, all their lives. They'd still be unable to smile, though, let alone laugh—if they did, they wouldn't be able to stop, and then they'd die.

I phoned my tutor and asked if there was really any such thing. He flew into a temper and yelled, If there isn't, then who wrote that essay on this topic for you, the one you turned in three months before graduation? I can't believe I taught a loser like you. Imagine ending up as a novelist!

I quickly hung up, then picked up the receiver again, meaning to call Lefty, but I couldn't make myself do it.

Nights in Yong'an City were always full of animal cries of no discernible origin. I was born here, and got used to it early on. My mother used to tell me, You can't be sure that beasts aren't people, or that people aren't just another type of beast.

Translated by Jeremy Tiang • Chinese | China

But that wasn't how things were. People would always be scared of beasts.

I put down the phone again. Someone was sobbing quietly, hugging me tightly and weeping. Someone was saying, Hello, hello, hello.

I lived alone on the seventeenth floor of Peach Blossom Villas, the Splendid River visible in the distance. My spacious apartment was empty, but still I heard crying. Stop that, I said.

But it continued.

●

The painter Lefty had gone a bit crazy. She kept phoning to tell me stories about her and that beast. I understood she had no one to talk to, and asked her, What do you want in return for these tales?

She didn't want anything, she already had everything, and she'd never get anything again.

Now and then, I'd see her in the papers. A beautiful painter will always have someone to love her. That young, wealthy human male, his eyes full of exuberance. On the phone, she sobbed, I've been getting these headaches recently, I'm always so confused, I don't know who I am.

This was because she couldn't find a sorrowful beast, the one who belonged to her. He'd been tamed by her, been with her, unspeaking, frequently silent, drawn to dark and damp places, fond of ice cream, sweet-natured, empty-eyed, preferring to go without clothes, to wander naked around the apartment—and she painted every one of his movements, the mesmerizing green patch on his belly that, somehow, seemed to be expanding.

His body was cool, which made it hard to keep your hands off him on summer nights. At times he let out a low moan, at times he spoke, but mostly he preferred the former. He was a beast. The scales on his leg gave off such a dazzling light.

Perhaps he really was the descendant of a poet, melancholy by nature.

I went back to the gallery where she'd held her exhibition, but all the portraits of Cloud had already been sold. I asked the owner who'd bought them. He stammered and refused to tell me, so I used Little Worm's name.

It was Mr. He, said the owner. He Qi.

He Qi. He Qi. I quickly found the face—I'd just seen him in the papers. He was Lefty's boyfriend, the famous Yong'an construction magnate's son.

●

Mr. He Qi turned out to be a reader of my books. I sat in his vast reception room, clutching a cup of Blue Mountain coffee, my attention somewhat unmoored. I asked him, Did you buy all the paintings of that beast?

Yes, he answered, nothing evasive about his beaming face.

Why? I asked.

I'm in love, he said, still smiling.

In love? I asked.

Yes, he said.

I hesitated. Do you mean with the beast, I said, or the painter?

He smiled, not responding.

He died, you know.

Who?

The beast.

Did he die? He didn't die. He didn't die, his soul is immortal.

I mean...

Does it really matter? I'm looking forward to your next novel.

●

The Pingle Cotton Mill was in the lower reaches of the Peacock River. It produced well-crafted blankets, bedsheets, and towels, to be shipped far and wide. Because the male beasts were so skilled with their hands, they held sway here, more or less dominating the market in Yong'an City. But their lives were hard, because the government imposed such high taxes on them. Little Worm whispered to me about what our leaders were saying behind the scenes. He claimed they were relying on the placid natures of the sorrowful beasts, otherwise there'd have been a revolt long ago!

At the entrance to Leye Estate was Yonas, the largest ice-cream distribution center. A group of young male beasts were there, staring at the shop. I asked one of them if he'd like a cone. He nodded eagerly.

I bought him an ice cream, and he happily started eating it. Sitting across from me, he said, Auntie, you're a good person.

I said, Why don't you call me Big Sister instead.

He obligingly switched, murmuring, Big Sister.

Translated by Jeremy Tiang • Chinese | China

I asked how old he was. He said five.

We sat in a little park outside Leye Estate. From a distance, the estate's walls were so covered in layers of ivy that you couldn't make out the buildings. Instead, they looked like countless enormous trees, phoenixes resting on their branches after long migrations.

What are you looking at? he asked.

I smiled, It's so pretty.

The little beast was startled. He said, What's that on your face?

A smile, I said.

Smile?

Yes.

Why can't I do that?

You can't smile, I told him, If you did, you would die.

I see, he said, How interesting. He looked relaxed, while it was I who felt uneasy. You call that a smile, but we call it pain, my daddy says, when the pain reaches its end, we'll die.

Would you like another ice cream? I said, trying to change the subject.

Yes, please.

I bought him another one, and he attacked it happily, until a long cry came from the distance, like a roar of nature.

He said he had to go home. Taking his leave, he said, Bye-bye Big Sister, you're such a nice person, when I'm grown up I'll marry you.

I smiled again, and said, You're too young, and you can't marry me, I'm human.

He said, I can, my daddy says it's possible, but if I did, you'd laugh.

Laugh?

He turned around, and his silhouette in the gloom was like a god. He said, That's right, or as you people would say, you'd die.

The next time I saw our resident troublemaker Little Worm at the Dolphin Bar, he had a different girlfriend. I said, Did you know He Qi bought all of Lefty's sorrowful beast paintings?

Little Worm looked sidelong at me and said, Of course I know. Why make such a big fuss over this? No wonder you've never amounted to anything.

He went on, I was the one who brought them together. He Qi saw those paintings and came pestering me for an introduction to Lefty. I gave him her phone number.

And then? I asked.

And then, and then the same old thing, He Qi called me up and said they'd finally met in person, and he was enchanted by the beast.

So it was the beast.

Yes. He Qi said, It's because I love him.

That night, Lefty phoned me. She and He Qi were sparking like crazy and she'd forgotten all about the beast. I said, a little angrily, I thought you were so in love with him.

She was quiet, then asked me, Is love possible between humans and beasts? Not the ones who marry rich men, go for surgery and hormone shots, believing themselves to be people. The ones who're still beasts. With humans. Can they be in love?

I love him, the painter concluded.

●

The sorrowful beasts already existed in ancient times. Thousands of years ago, they came south to Yong'an City. Yong'an is a four-sided place, full of flying sand to the south and west, warm and damp to the north and east—so they settled in the northeast, an isolated community that married off its attractive females to the highest bidders, splitting the proceeds forty-sixty with the local government. As our city acquired skyscrapers and elevated highways, they continued living in their dilapidated estate, at peace with the world, placid and mild.

When I was in college, my tutor said, All beasts have a beastly nature. Please take care around them.

I phoned him and told him about my latest discoveries. He said earnestly, Don't dig any further, it won't do you any good.

I said, No, I want to know how he died.

My tutor sighed. You're still as stubborn as ever. There are things it's better to forget.

But I couldn't forget this. The night before graduation, my tutor brought me to see his collection of specimen beasts, soaking in long vitrines, their

Translated by Jeremy Tiang • Chinese | China

faces human. I remembered the male sorrowful beast. The green patch on his belly had been cut open, and inside were two rows of tightly packed teeth, a space in between them. My tutor said, That's his true mouth. His beastly mouth.

I couldn't stop retching. I dashed out of the lab, and never went back in.

Every beast has a beastly nature. At the full moon, human children ought to stay at home. My mother would say, The beasts all want to eat people, just like people eat them.

Mutual destruction is the only way to survive. That's the circle of life. That's truth.

But scientists said they'd invented and put out a brand-new hormone that could completely suppress the beastly nature of female sorrowful beasts. Even on full-moon nights, they'd no longer make their bird-like cries.

They held clinical trials, and the results were undeniably successful. The drug went into mass production, with a hefty price tag—after all, the wives of rich men had someone to foot the bill. Little Worm was outraged, yelling, This disrupts the ecological equilibrium! His new girlfriend gazed worshipfully at him.

I took a deep drag on my cigarette. It was easy to imagine that after many years, Yong'an would have no beasts left, all of them dead from the hormones, completely controlled, filled with humanity, passing among skyscrapers, leaping between elevators, getting match-made then married, reproducing but stopping at one child, never mind if it's a boy or girl.

When that time came, all novelists would have hormone injections too, turning us into computer programmers, and all zoologists would undergo surgery to become bus conductors. Everyone would give up their research into the nonexistent, and there'd be no myths, no beasts, no history, no fantasy. The government would rattle along, printing money. Yong'an would truly become an international metropolis.

Therefore, historians of the future ought to thank the female beast Rain. She was allergic to the hormone shots, which turned her skin bright red, leaving her screeching endlessly. Most Yong'an residents saw this horrifying scene on TV, her skin so red it was almost transparent, the human fetus dimly visible through the bare skin of her belly, her hair in disarray as she ran naked through the streets, the TV station's van careening after her.

People saw a terrified, tormented sorrowful beast, and just like the little beast said to me, she was smiling. Sorrowful beasts don't smile from joy, but only because of sadness, because of pain. Once they start, it's impossible to stop, not until they die.

Her smile was so beautiful, even I wept for her. The whole city was captivated. As she sprinted, she shrieked like a bird—the old people said, they'd die without regrets, having lived to see the smile of a sorrowful beast.

She smiled down the entire length of Yanhe Street, then climbed the statue of the ancient hero in Victory Square. Her fetus stared helplessly through the reddish translucent skin of her belly.

She let out a final, shattering cry, her smile as dazzling as the peach blossoms. Everyone nearby said seeing her was like looking upon a goddess.

She died. Once sorrowful beasts smiled, they died.

●

Production of the new hormone was stopped. The sorrowful beasts of Leye Estate went on a protest march, roaring as they walked down the street. Humans ducked out of their way, terrified. The mayor came forward to speak. He offered his apologies, and arranged a funeral for the female beast Rain, the most lavish one ever seen.

On TV, her husband sobbed heartrendingly, his shoulders heaving. A moving sight. Little Worm brought me to the funeral. Outside the ceremonial hall, we ran into the painter Lefty and He Qi.

Lefty looked at me with a strange expression. She was even lovelier than ever, but so fragile, unsmiling, her expression pensive, her figure frail. He Qi clutched her hand tightly.

None of us said a word about Cloud, only nodded somberly and went inside. Lefty wanted to see Rain's body. He Qi held her back, but she said, I want to take a last look, I didn't take good care of her.

He Qi said, Don't go over there, it'll make you sad.

No one could have expected what happened next.

Lefty ran over like a madwoman, shoved the coffin lid open, and stared at the body inside. She reached out, as if to touch her, but before making contact, she smiled.

It was a radiant smile, and everyone was momentarily enchanted. Little

Translated by Jeremy Tiang • Chinese | China

Worm, standing beside me, let out a very male sound, a meaningless sigh.

She was smiling, and so she couldn't stop. He Qi stumbled over to tug at her, saying, You mustn't smile, she's already dead, don't smile!

He wept, and still she smiled. He said, I love you so much, please don't leave me, it cost so much for us to be together, stop smiling!

Still smiling, she let out a peal of proud, beautiful birdsong. Her voice rose up, startling everyone present.

Then she died.

And that was how the painter Lefty met her end.

In Yong'an City's Dolphin Bar, one often ran into the resident busybody Little Worm. His most recent piece of gossip had to do with the painter Lefty and her sorrowful beast.

> *They'd thought they could be together, but in the end, it lasted no longer than flowers in a mirror, the moon reflected in water.*

The way he told it, the government carried out an autopsy on her corpse, and in her belly, which was still faintly green, they found the teeth that hadn't yet broken down, and the half-digested remains of the real Lefty's body.

My tutor phoned to scold me. He said, I told you not to dig any deeper, I warned you. Then he asked, Should I come and see you? I said, No need.

Much later, I ran into He Qi at a party. He'd grown more feeble-looking. Pulling at my arm, he asked, You've written so many stories, you tell me, can humans and beasts love each other? Can they be together?

I felt cold all over, and suddenly thought of the painter Lefty, or perhaps by then she was already the sorrowful beast Cloud, asking me sadly on the telephone, Can humans and beasts love each other? Is it possible? I love him, she'd said.

I'd once thought I knew the whole of this story. I thought it was him and her. Who'd have guessed it was a tragedy of him and him? They'd thought they could be together, but in the end, it lasted no longer than flowers in a mirror, the moon reflected in water. It ended because her smile was so beautiful.

The sorrowful beasts lived in the northeastern quarter of Yong'an City. Uncorrupted by nature, they preferred the cold. Since ancient time, no calamity had stopped them. At the full moon, the female beasts let out long mating calls. It was easy to produce male sorrowful beasts but not female, for on nights when the moon was full, a male was able to mate with a human woman, and at the moment of greatest joy, open his green belly-mouth wide and swallow her whole. He'd then take on her likeness, slowly digesting her consciousness, finally becoming a new female beast, and so reproducing, generation after generation.

These beasts were faithful, and only sought one mate in life. But they never smiled. If they did, they would die—hence their name, sorrowful.

Translated by Jeremy Tiang • Chinese | China

Техника

Събират се покрай бараките
край складовете слушат музика
разговарят танцуват
подготвят се.

Сутрин когато стават за работа
някои от тях дъхтят на алкохол
други гледат с класово презрение.

Започват първите заплахи:
блъскаш се в стена
тя ти отвръща с непознати лозунги

галиш цвете то ти се смее
гледаш небето минава робот
и го покрива с пушек.

В града замръкват почернели машини
и цяла нощ гризат от глад асфалта.

В планините все още е тихо
Балканът пее хайдушка песен
а нейде в полето
денонощно роботите жънат.

Translated by
DIMITER KENAROV

Machinery

They hang around by the shanties
by the warehouses they listen to music
they talk they dance
they're getting ready.

When they get up for work in the morning
some reek of booze
others look around with class hatred.

The first danger appears:
you hit a wall
and it answers you back with alien slogans

you pat a flower and it laughs at you
you look at the sky and a robot zips by
covering all with smoke.

Darkness descends over blackened machines in the city
and all night they hungrily gnaw on asphalt.

It's still quiet in the mountains
the Balkan is singing a rebel song
and somewhere in the fields
round the clock the robots reap.

Translated by Dimiter Kenarov • Bulgarian | Bulgaria

Vita nuova

Те живеят спокойно. Ръфат бурми.
Галят майка си—поточната машина.
Тя ражда техни братя на всеки пет минути:
някои от тях са кораби
други—роботи.

Корабите започват да плуват.
Роботите започват да ходят.

Как живееш ти днес
приятелю мой робот?
беше време потресно
по-друг беше живота.

Ти сега имаш всичко
твойте устни са пълни
като млада горичка
радост в тебе покълва

из небето отровно
ти подскачаш свободно!

Vita Nuova

They live quietly. Nibble on screws.
They caress their mother—the conveyer belt.
She births their brothers every five minutes:
some of them are ships
others are robots.

The ships begin to sail.
The robots start walking.

How do you do now
robot my old friend?
Times used to appall
and life was different.

Now you have everything
your lips are full
like young saplings
joy sprouts in you

through poisoned skies
you bounce and rejoice!

Translated by Dimiter Kenarov • Bulgarian | Bulgaria

Каменни въглища

Вие мислите: там, под земята,
там ще можем да бъдем добри.
Ще работим из предприятията,
ще натрупаме доста пари,
докато дойдат жената, децата.

И си мислите: колко е просто,
черно слънце отгоре блести,
а отдолу с естествена доблест
цветни руди разтварят очи
като мъж след прекарана болест.

Всъщност ето как: слизаш надолу,
цял живот си мечтал за жени,
облечени в дрехи от алкохол, и—
изведнъж гледаш—времето спи
върху купчина блудкава тор…

Ще си кажеш тогава: живота бе дим!
Нека с вечното днес са се съединим.
Да сънуваме розови сънища,
докато ставаме каменни въглища!

Lumps of Coal

You think: there under the ground,
There we can all be high class,
We'll work in factory compounds
And we'll make tons of cash
Till wives and kids come around.

And you think: such a simple thing,
Up there a black sun shines
While beneath, with natural strength,
Precious ores open their eyes
Like a man convalescing.

The truth is: you descend in the dark
Dreaming your whole life of chicks
Wearing outfits of booze. Hark!
Suddenly you notice that time ticks
On mounds of featureless dung.

Then you'll proclaim: life is shit!
Let's merge today with the infinite!
And dream our pink-laced rigmarole
As we turn into lumps of coal!

KIM MIN JEONG is an award-winning
poet and editor. Her work is unique in
its use of playfulness and language that isn't
considered literary or "womanly." While many
other contemporary Korean feminist poets
disrupt gender constructions by exploring
the grotesque or by rewriting mythology,
Kim Min Jeong's poems use humor to lighten
the burden of the gendered sex.

빨강에
고하다

빨강구두

네가 사준 빨강구두를 처음 신었다
네가 아는 내 애인과 오락실에 갔다
Dance Dance Revolution!
스텝 틀어져 발이 밟혀 죽겠는데
왜 자꾸 내 이름은 부른다니?
시선을 내리깐 너는 거기 그렇게 서 있었고
환연오락실 카운터에 너는 동전 바꾸는 손이었다
미안해, 불륜 중이야!

Translated by
JI YOON LEE AND JAKE LEVINE

Red,
an Announcement

Red Shoes

I wore the red shoes you bought me for the first time.

With my lover who you know, I went to the arcade.

Dance Dance Revolution!

Whenever I miss a step and stomp your foot to death

Why do you repeatedly call my name?

With a lowered glance, you are standing there

At the welcome counter of the arcade,

The hand exchanging coins.

Sorry. I'm in the middle of having an affair!

빨강팬티

네가 손만 잡고 잠만 자자고 했다
네가 아는 내 애인이 고해성사를 한 직후였다
Eli Eli Lema Sabachtani!
코 골며 꿈속으로 나자빠진 줄 알았는데
왜 자꾸 내 이름은 부른다니?
빨강팬티에다 나는 날개형 화이트를 대고 있었고
화장실 변기 위에 나는 오래 저린 엉덩이였다
미안해, 생리 중이야!

빨강무

네가 솟고 있는 이 욕구가 뭘까 내게 물었다
네가 아는 내 애인은 유부남에 발기부전이라 예뻤다
a hundred miles, a hundred miles...
세 번은 더 불러야 *five hundred miles*인데
왜 자꾸 내 이름은 부른다니?
발가벗은 채로 나는 문밖 조간신문을 집고 있었고
눈 마주친 옆집 남자는 내게 물린 빨강무였다
미안해, 식사 중이야!

Red Panties

Right after my lover who you know made his confession
Eli Eli Lema Sabachtani!
You said let's just hold hands and go to sleep.
Even though you snored and I could have swore you fell into a dream
Why do you repeatedly call my name?
Underneath my red panties, I am wearing a white winged pad and
Because I sat on the toilet in the bathroom too long, my ass is numb.

Sorry. I'm in the middle of my period!

Red Radish

You asked me, what the hell is this swelling desire?
Because he was married and impotent
My lover, who you know, was an absolutely lovely man.
a hundred miles, a hundred miles...
you've got to say it three more times, to *five hundred miles*, and yet
why is it that you continually call my name?
Without wearing clothes, I went outside to grab the morning paper and
Made eye contact with the man who is my next-door neighbor
Who, let's face it, was a red radish I bit into.

Sorry. I am eating!

Translated by Ji Yoon Lee and Jake Levine • Korean | South Korea

젖이라는 이름의 좆

네게 좆이 있다면
내겐 젖이 있다
그러니 과시하지 마라
유치하다면
시작은 다 너로부터 비롯함일지니

어쨌거나 우리 쥐면 한 손이라는 공통점
어쨌거나 우리 빨면 한 입이라는 공통점
어쨌거나 우리 빨면 한 접시라는 공통점

(아, 난 유방암으로 한쪽 가슴을 도려냈다고!
이 지극한 공평, 이 아찔한 안도)

섹스를 나눈 뒤
등을 맞대고 잠든 우리
저마다의 심장을 향해 도넛처럼,
완전 도-우-넛처럼 잔뜩 오그라들 때
저기 침대 위에 큼지막하게 던져진

두 짝의 가슴이,
두 쪽의 불알이,

어머 착해

Tits Named Dick

You've got dick,
And I've got tits, however
don't make it a spectacle.
If you think that's childish
Remember it's from you where things originated.

Anyway, a point we share is that when we grab, we hold one hand.
Anyway, a point we share is that when we suck lips, we suck one set.
Anyway, a point we share is that when we chop, we use one plate.

(Ah, they scooped out one of my cancerous tits. Harsh equality,
  dizzying relief.)

After splitting the sex up
Dos-à-dos, we sleep
In the direction of our respective hearts, like donuts,
Really like do-ugh-nuts, curling heavily atop the bed
Vastly cast

Two tits
Two balls

How lovely!

Translated by Ji Yoon Lee and Jake Levine • Korean | South Korea

피날레

혁대로 내 목을 조이는 걸
그저 바라만 보고 있으니까
그는 떠났다

한 시인이 닭에게 그러했듯
나를 먹을 수는 있었으나
나를 잡을 수는 없었던
예민한 그였기 때문이리라

그리고 오늘,
그의 뒷주머니에 선물로 찔러 넣었던
오른손이 되돌아왔다

왼손보다 양옆으로 약 3센티미터가량
손바닥이 자라 있었다 손톱 또한
오렌지를 살찌우는 뜨거운 태양 아래
즙을 내기 좋은 고깔처럼 다듬어진 뒤였다

닭살을 긁은 뒤 울긋불긋 솟은
살진 여드름을 짜기에 더없이 좋았으므로
나는 내 안의 작디작은 죽음을 잊었다

그렇게 흔들흔들
안녕 새로운 나여

Finale

As the belt tightened around my neck
I merely stared
So he up and left.

As a poet might treat a chicken,
He could eat me
But he couldn't slaughter me
Because he was a delicate man.

And today,
My right hand that I gifted
By thrusting it in his back pocket
Has suddenly come back.

Both long and wide, the right palm has grown
3 centimeters in size bigger than the left. And the nails!
Well trimmed like cones good for juicing
Beneath the hot, orange-plumping sun.

They were perfect for
Popping the fleshy pimples that thrust up willy-nilly
After I scraped off the chicken skin,
So I forgot the itty-bitty death in me.

Yeah, that's how I shake it.
Say hello to the new me!

Translated by Ji Yoon Lee and Jake Levine • Korean | South Korea

One of Spain's most famous writers, ANA MARÍA MATUTE (1925–2014) was awarded the prestigious Cervantes Prize in 2010. According to Mario Vargas Llosa, she is "one of the most important writers in the Spanish language."

El bosque

El bosque empezaba detrás de la casa, y casi nadie iba allí. La niebla se acercaba tanto que borraba las copas de los árboles y entonces todo aparecía íntimo y secreto, tan cerrado y pegado al suelo que la obligaba a permanecer horas y horas entre los troncos, en el húmedo velo, sin deseo alguno de volver a la casa.

Nadie entendía esto, y la madre, la abuela, y los hermanos solían mirarla con severidad: "¿Por qué has tardado tanto? ¿Dónde estuviste?"

En el bosque vivían árboles de varias razas, pero ella amaba sobre todos los demás a los robles. En sus troncos había túneles que conducían por desconocidas galerías hacia el interior de la tierra. A menudo acercaba los ojos a aquellos agujeros, y contemplaba la fosforescente oscuridad. También le gustaba perderse en las altas hierbas, entre los helechos azulados. Buscaba la venenosa maraubina, el arzadú, y, llegado el otoño, las cabezas moradas y misteriosas de los despachapastores; y en lo más umbrío, fresas silvestres y frambuesas. A nadie hablaba de esto. A menudo perdía cosas: . . .

Translated by
ROBERT S. RUDDER

The Forest

The forest began behind the house, and hardly anyone went there. The mist hung so low that it shrouded the treetops: then everything seemed intimate and secret. So closed off and anchored to the ground that it invited her to stay among the trunks for hours and hours, in the damp veil, having no desire at all to return home.

No one understood this. And the mother, the grandmother, and the brothers and sisters only looked at her sternly: "Why are you so late? Where have you been?"

Several different kinds of trees were in the forest, but she loved the oaks more than all the rest. In their trunks were tunnels that led through unknown galleries, deep down into the earth. Often she would put her eyes up to those holes and gaze at the phosphorescent darkness. She liked to lose herself in the tall grasses too, among the azure ferns. She sought out the poisonous maraubina, the arzadú; and when autumn arrived, the dark and mysterious heads of the meadow saffron, and in the shadiest part, wild

Translated by Robert S. Rudder • Spanish | Spain

strawberries and raspberries. She told no one about this. Often she lost things: handkerchiefs, belts, and once, one of her shoes. When she was in bed she liked to imagine that her things were making their way through the forest: handkerchiefs with her initials on them, that shoe without laces, half sunken in the wet, warm ground, searching for rivers. Like strange boats that would find an infinity of living things on their journey, looking at them, but not understanding them. They belonged to her (her handkerchiefs, her pencils, her shoe also), and they would travel forever through the interior of the forest. It was comforting to think of that. They would not change.

She did not need the love of the others, or their house, or their dishes, or their glasses. Or the words that slipped out through their teeth, like tiny snakes.

Because she became afraid when she saw that silver shoe in the glass cabinet, an exact reproduction of the one her mother wore as a child: hard and shiny, holding the impression of a baby's foot. Her mother's name was engraved on the sole, along with a date. She hated that shoe in the horrible glass cabinet in the living room. As horrible as the dining room, with its enormous walnut table, and its tall, dark hutches. That was where the cutlery rattled against the dishes, and the water and wine plashed while it was being poured into the glasses. She closed her eyes and escaped to the forest where there were no partridges or heads of stuffed boar with their glassy yellow eyes.

"The forest is treacherous, its ground is insidious. There are snakes and vermin wandering around out there," said the grandmother.

They thought about selling it, but it wasn't good even for that. The things around her might be very meaningful to the others, but not to her. She knew only one thing. The world was divided into two parts. Herself, and the others.

The mother was always telling her: "You're bad. I knew it the minute you were born. You're bad; you're not like your brothers and sisters."

They said that she was very pretty at first, but there was always something odd about her: she had the dark eyes and skin of the rest of the family. But her hair—it was yellow.

"What a strange child," said the grandmother, as she ran her fingers—laden with rings—through her hair. Then her hair began to turn dark, and finally it ended up looking black. But they still kept saying: "How strange."

Some who saw her shook their heads. The nanny and the washer women, when they saw her running along the river's edge, shook their fists at her from a distance, and shouted things that she did not understand. She would only look at the others out of the corner of her eye. She could read into everyone's heart very well. And a little voice inside her said: "You don't fool me."

Soon she was no longer pretty. Her sisters were like reeds. Her brothers, obedient, good. Not her.

There was a dog in the house named Lucio. He looked at her a great deal, and sometimes he followed her. But he knew that those escapades were severely punished, and he did not dare go with her very often. She knew, in spite of his cowardice, that Lucio loved her.

"You shouldn't love me," she told him. "The others should not love me."

Because she had heard the mother say to the grandmother:

"This one is going to bring misfortune to anyone who loves her. She's one of those who carry harm with them wherever they go. I don't know how she can be a child of mine."

She did not need the love of the others, or their house, or their dishes, or their glasses. Or the words that slipped out through their teeth, like tiny snakes. Sometimes she would lie under the table and listen to what they were saying, until they discovered her: "Look at her, listening to things she shouldn't. She's wicked!"

Even the grandmother said: "This one doesn't love anybody."

And it was true. Not even Lucio. She was the only good one: she was the forest, the trees, the river.

Early in the afternoon it was the time for the river. The sun left sticky gold on the stones. She went there to smudge her hands and her legs. She would sit down and daub her knees, which were round and very beautiful. It was the same gold that covered the wings of butterflies. She knew a song that she would sing very softly so that no one could hear.

"What are you laughing at?"

She was silent. The mother said: "When you narrow your eyes, you're the very picture of evil."

She had to get out of the house, take herself far away from the glass case and the grandmother's hard fingers, threaded with rings that

Translated by Robert S. Rudder • Spanish | Spain

were too large, dancing, making a sound like bones clicking together. When the grandmother's hands, flecked with spots the color of clay, rested on her head they dug their icy, golden rings into her. She also put on the ones the grandfather had worn when he was alive, and one of them had an ivory facing and was probably bewitched.

The house had high ceilings, and Venetian blinds full of cracks that let the splintered sun come in. Every sound found its way through those cracks, along with the air and the warm wind of summer.

"What could this girl be seeing in the forest?"

She saw many things. One day she sat on the ground and saw a theater. It was between two tree trunks. There was a beautiful red curtain and several dolls taking bows.

"I want a doll," she said.

But they paid her no attention, and she had to wait for her birthday to come. They took her to the city in the car. They walked through one store after another, and finally they told her: "Choose your present."

There was no doll there like the one she wanted. When they got back, she made one in the forest, with twigs and colored rags that the nanny gave her. She tied a cord onto it, and dragged it around behind her. From time-to-time she looked at how it would bend the grass under its weight. It was very beautiful. She named it *Timbuktu*, like a city she had read about somewhere.

Lucio immediately became jealous of Timbuktu, and one night, while she was asleep, he tore it apart with his teeth.

She found its remnants near the river, and while hiding in the rushes she cried bitterly. That opened a void inside her, and many times she would walk through the forest, calling for Timbuktu. Lucio felt very ashamed, and he avoided her. And yet, she had no ill feelings toward him.

Even more, one day she went over to him and began to pet him.

"Why are you petting Lucio? Oh, what a muddleheaded girl!" the servants remarked.

Under her fingers, Lucio closed his eyes, and his eyelids, full of wrinkles, like the grandmother's, trembled with emotion, or perhaps with fear.

The next day they found Lucio dead, at the door to her bedroom. She got up, barefoot, when she heard the servants crying out. Her mother came, along with her older brothers and sisters and even the grandmother, pounding on the floor with her cane. The mother stared at her: "Did you do something to him?"

"I was petting him."

That created quite a commotion, and they asked her many questions. She grew tired of answering, and with her silence they all began to have suspicions.

"You killed him, and you're going to be sorry," said the oldest brother, his eyes filled with angry tears.

It was useless to tell them: "He loved me so much that he died after I petted him. He couldn't go on living one more day after he knew that I was being good to him, that I wasn't mad at him because of Timbuktu."

> *She kept calling out for Timbuktu on days when it was foggy, or when it was raining.*

Since they could find out nothing further, they finally left her alone. She kept calling out for Timbuktu on days when it was foggy, or when it was raining. The rain was very good. She went to the highest part of the house, all the way up to the window of the granary. From there she could see the garden very well. Water was falling very hard on the ground. It was springtime, and heavy showers poured down, and from below a sharp smell burst forth that filled the air like music. The earth grew darker and darker, until it took on the color of blood, and the leaves turned a very brilliant green. Some plants looked black, and others dark blue. Puddles formed, and the sun turned red behind the poplars, across the river. She liked that almost as much as going into the forest, and she whispered softly: "Timbuktu."

They buried Lucio beyond the planted fields. She knew the exact spot because the eldest brother marked it with a limestone rock, and the ground looked freshly stirred. She made a little garden over his grave, with small furrows, and she planted seeds. Every day she went to see if the pale green heads of her plants were showing. But days passed, and finally she forgot about it. (Long afterward, when she no longer remembered anything about it, she walked on that spot, and it seemed to her that the ground had turned gray, with an ashen tone, and she felt a sharp stab of pain inside herself.) Sometimes these unknown things, full of darkness, came upon her unexpectedly.

Like her brothers and sisters, she wore a round gold medallion that hung from her neck. When she ran a long while, and then dropped to the ground

Translated by Robert S. Rudder • Spanish | Spain

among the big trees in the forest, the medallion, hanging from its chain like a gold communion wafer, bounced against her chest. The sun drew a hard, sharp sheen from it, and she had to close her eyes because she was afraid. The medallion was hot then, damp with sweat, and she touched it as if it were an alien being, looking at her. It wasn't like her shoes that were her very own, and that she loved. And she would have taken no pleasure in knowing that her medallion, if it were lost, would go wandering underground. Because the ground would do nothing with it, and it could appear any day intact, hard and yellow, just as it went away. The earth would not go inside it, the way it would her. And while lying there, she let one arm go limp on the ground and felt as though she were sinking down into it, and she knew that a slow pain would gradually overcome her and carry her off.

She thought about the dead. She would go out and look at the crosses in the cemetery, the white flowers of the brambles, next to the abandoned graves. She thought about the dead because they were there, down below, and they could peer out from inside, putting their eyes next to the dark mouths of the trees. They would look at the sun's stars, scattered here and there among the ferns; the rain that left everything shining, as blinding as a moonlit night. They would see it all from inside, the way it should be seen, without having to go wandering here and there, looking into the tunnels of tree trunks. Then she felt sorry for herself, her head leaning on one of the oaks, letting her tears slide slowly down, like something beautiful and fleeting, in the rays of the sun.

Belgian-born HENRI MICHAUX
(1899–1984) was both a poet and a painter.
The three texts translated here are taken
from his 1930 collection, *A Certain Plume*, in
which Kafka and Klee meet the Marx Brothers
in the adventures of Monsieur Plume—Mr.
Quill Pen.

Naisssance

Pon naquit d'un œuf, puis il naquit d'une morue et en naissant la fit éclater, puis il naquit d'un soulier; par bipartition, le soulier plus petit à gauche, et lui à droite, puis il naquit d'une feuille de rhubarbe, en même temps qu'un renard; le renard et lui se regardèrent un instant puis filèrent chacun de leur côté. Ensuite il naquit d'un cafard, d'un œil de langouste, d'une carafe; d'une otarie et il lui sortit par les moustaches, d'un têtard et il lui sortit du derrière, d'une jument et il lui sortit par les naseaux, puis il versait des larmes en cherchant les mamelles, car il ne venait au monde que pour téter. Puis il naquit d'un trombone et le trombone le nourrit pendant treize mois, puis il fut sevré et confié au sable qui s'étendait partout, car c'était le désert. Et seul le fils du trombone peut se nourrir dans le désert, seul avec le chameau. Puis il naquit d'une femme et il fut grandement étonné, et réfléchissant sur son sein, il suçotait, il crachotait, il ne savait plus quoi; il remarqua ensuite que c'était une femme, quoique personne ne lui eût jamais fait la moindre allusion à ce sujet; il commençait à lever la tête, tout seul, à la regarder d'un petit œil perspicace, mais la perspicacité n'était qu'une lueur, l'étonnement était bien plus grand et, vu son âge, son grand plaisir était quand même de faire glou glou glou, et de se rencoigner sur le sein, vitre exquise, et de suçoter.

Il naquit d'un zèbre, il naquit d'une truie, il naquit d'une guenon empaillée, une jambe accrochée à un faux cocotier et l'autre pendant, il en sortit plein d'une odeur d'étoupe et se mit à brailler et à siffler dans le bureau du

Translated by
RICHARD SIEBURTH

Birth

Pon was born of an egg, then he was born of a cod which, once born, he proceeded to explode, then he was born of a shoe, bipartite, the shoe being smaller to the left with him to the right, then he was born of a rhubarb leaf and, at the same time, of a fox; the fox and he glared at each other for a moment, then raced off in their respective directions. Then he was born of a cockroach, of the eye of a lobster, of a carafe, of a sea lion from whose moustaches he emerged, of a tadpole from whose rump he emerged, from a mare from whose nostrils he emerged, shedding tears as he searched for her teats, having come into the world with only one thing on his mind: to suckle. Then he was born of a trombone and the trombone nursed him for thirteen months, at which point he was weaned and scattered to the sands which stretched far and wide, for this was the desert. And only the son of a trombone can find nourishment in the desert, alone with the camel. Then he was born of a woman and was most astounded and, lost in thought upon her breast, he sucked, he spat up, he was confused; he soon came to realize that this was a woman, even though nobody had ever informed him of the fact; he began to raise his head, all on his own, to spy at her intently, but this intentness of gaze was but a dim awareness, his astonishment was far greater and, given his age, his greatest pleasure was simply to go glu-glu-glu and to nestle into her breast, this exquisite pane of glass, and proceed to suck.

He was born of a zebra, he was born of a sow, he was born of a stuffed she-monkey, one of her legs attached to a fake coconut tree, the other

Translated by Richard Sieburth • French | France

naturaliste qui s'élança sur lui avec le dessein évident de l'empailler, mais il lui fit faux bond et naquit dans un parfait silence d'un fœtus qui se trouvait au fond d'un bocal, il lui sortit de la tête, une énorme tête spongieuse plus douce qu'un utérus où il mijota son affaire pendant plus de trois semaines, puis il naquit lestement d'une souris vivante, car il fallait se presser, le naturaliste ayant eu vent de quelque chose; puis il naquit d'un obus qui éclata en l'air; puis se sentant toujours observé, il trouva le moyen de naître d'une frégate et passa l'océan sous ses plumes, puis dans la première île venue naquit dans le premier être venu et c'était une tortue, mais comme il grandissait il s'aperçut que c'était le moyeu d'un ancien fiacre transporté là par des colons portugais. Alors il naquit d'une vache, c'est plus doux, puis d'un lézard géant de la Nouvelle-Guinée, gros comme un âne, puis il naquit pour la seconde fois d'une femme, et faisant cela il songeait à l'avenir, car c'est encore les femmes qu'il connaissait le mieux, et avec lesquelles plus tard il serait le plus à l'aise, et déjà maintenant regardait cette poitrine si douce et pleine, en faisant les petites comparaisons que lui permettait son expérience déjà longue.

hanging free, he emerged smelling of oakum and proceeded to bawl and whistle in the office of a naturalist who threw himself onto him with the obvious intent of taxidermizing him, but he managed to elude him and was born in perfect silence from a fetus lodged in the bottom of a jar, he emerged from its head, a huge spongy head sweeter than a uterus, where he let the whole matter simmer for more than three weeks, then he was briskly born from a white mouse, for he was in a rush, given that the naturalist had caught wind of something; then he was born of a mortar that burst into the air; then, feeling that he was still under the gun, he managed to be born from a frigate bird and winged his way across the seas beneath its feathers, and then on the first island on which he landed he was born from the first creature he encountered and it was a tortoise, but as he grew ever larger he realized that it was the hub of the wheel of an ancient coach that been deposited there by Portuguese colonists. So he was born of a cow, far more pleasant, then of a giant New Guinea lizard as large as a donkey, then for the second time he was born of a woman and, so doing, dreamed of the future, given that it was women whom he after all knew the best of all and with whom he would later be most at ease, and he was now already looking upon this breast, so tender, so plump, making such small comparisons as his extensive experience now allowed.

Translated by Richard Sieburth • French | France

Première mort
de Plume

"Assurément," lui disait la maîtresse de maison, "vous ne dansez pas mal. Seulement vous faite des pas tellement grands. Voyez, tout le monde nous regarde. Mais puisque vous ne m'écoutez pas, mon mari, je présume, sera bien aise de venir vous parler plutôt avec l'épée, demain matin."

Plume se mordit les lèvres, la reconduisit et prit congé froidement.

Mais comme il allait sortir, l'attaché militaire du Danemark le prit par la manche. "Je vous en prie, ma fille a si rarement l'occasion de parler danois. Elle sera certainement ravie de vous accorder une danse."

Il l'invita donc, et ils dansèrent. Tout à coup le fiancé les sépara violemment.

"Écoutez, emportez-la plutôt chez vous tout de suite, si c'est pour la tenir ainsi. Vous recevrez mes témoins demain à dix heures, monsieur."

Plume reconduisit la jeune fille, salua et sortit. Qu'est-ce qui se passe ce soir? pensait-il. Je n'ai même pas regardé ces femmes et je dois me battre pour elles.

Tout à coup une dame qui était près de l'entrée du vestiaire s'approcha de lui. "Voilà une heure que je vous cherche." Son mari la suivait. "J'en ai assez entendu, dit-il. Préparez-vous à mourir tous les deux."

Alors Plume absolument furieux sortit ses revolvers, fit feu sur lui et rentrant dans la salle, abattit tous les homes présents.

Il fut ensuite pris d'une grande lassitude. Ce qui le soulageait surtout, c'était de penser que le lendemain il n'aurait pas de témoins à recevoir. Il n'aimait pas attendre du monde chez lui.

La maîtresse de maison s'approcha et lui dit, "Il reste mes domestiques." Et avant qu'il eût pu faire un geste, les valets l'attrapèrent, l'étendirent à terre, et lui tapèrent dessus tant qu'ils purent.

Puis la comtesse dit, "Maintenant, dansez." Il lui fallait danser avec les femmes sans aucune interruption puisqu'il était seul cavalier. Parfois il

First Death of Plume

No doubt about it, said the lady of the house, You're not a bad dancer. Except that your steps are so wide. As you can see, everybody is staring at us. But since you refuse to listen to me, I suspect that tomorrow morning my husband will be most willing to address you with a rapier instead.

Plume bit his lips, accompanied her back to her seat, and coldly took his leave.

But as he was about to depart, the military attaché of Denmark grabbed him by the sleeve. I beg of you, my daughter so rarely gets the opportunity to speak Danish. She would be most delighted to grant you a dance.

He proceeded to invite her, and they danced. All of a sudden, her fiancé violently pulled them apart.

Listen, if you're going to hold her this tight, why not just take her home with you right off the bat? You'll be hearing from my seconds tomorrow at ten o'clock, Monsieur.

Plume escorted the young girl back to her seat, bowed, and withdrew. What on earth is going on tonight? he thought. I did not so much as cast a glance at these women and here I am, having to engage in duels for their sake.

A woman who was hovering by the entrance to the cloakroom suddenly came up to him. I've been looking all over for you for an hour. Her husband was close behind. I've heard enough, he said. Prepare to die, both of you.

At which point Plume could not contain his anger. Pulling out his revolvers, he shot the husband dead and then returned to the ballroom where he mowed down every single man in sight.

He was now overcome with fatigue. But what relieved him the most was the thought that he would not have to receive the seconds the following morning. He hated waiting for visitors at home.

The lady of the house came up to him and said, My servants are

Translated by Richard Sieburth • French | France

tombait par terre. Alors elles le piétinaient. Sa figure ne ressemblait plus à rien quand les agents entèrent. Et l'ayant pris pour la victime: Qui accusez-vous? luis dirent-ils.

"Mme C... (c'était la maîtresse de maison).

— Quels sont vos témoins?

— Hélas, dit-il, elle les a tués. Voyez, ils sont tous là derrière les fauteuils.

— Ça, c'est vraiment jouer de malheur, disaient-ils, avoir tant de témoins et les perdre aussitôt."

Et ils conduisirent Plume à l'hôpital. Il n'y avait plus de place. Puis dans un autre. C'était un hôpital militaire.

"Encore un de ces fameux mutilés de la face, criait le médecin-major, qui, parce qu'il a le nez de travers, se croit déjà réformé. Demain à 5 heures, vous repartirez, mon garçon. Inscrivez," disait-il à l'infirmier. "Il fait partie du convoi de demain pour le front. Au suivant."

Mme C..., qui voulait montrer du zèle, était infirmière de garde cette nuit à l'hôpital. Plume l'aperçut à temps.

Un de nous deux, dit-il, va passer un mauvais quart d'heure. Que le ciel au moins une fois me vienne en aide. S'étant introduit dans la pharmacie, il prit un bocal de teinture d'iode qui en contenait bien un litre et demi et ayant vivement bâillonné Mme C... avec son mouchoir, il se mit à lui inonder la tête et la figure de la teinture d'iode (par le mouchoir le liquide pénétrait aussi dans la bouche et sur la langue, la rendant comme du bois). Il lui en versait également dans les oreilles et dans les yeux. Il ouvrait les yeux de force.

"Ça pique un peu," disait-il. "Mais c'est souverain. Allons, ne faites pas la mijaurée. Le corps medical est unanime à recommander le produit."

Et la teinture coulait. Quand on découvrit l'affreuse tête de momie, le lendemain, le coupable était loin, il gisait sur une route du Nord, le ventre ouvert par un obus, et il avait un sourire bizarre, le sourire triste mais si paisible qu'il avait souvent lorsqu'il était en vie.

still on duty. And before he could make the slightest move, the butlers seized hold of him, wrestled him to the ground, and beat the daylights out of him.

Then the countess said, Now dance! Since there were no other gentlemen remaining, he had to dance with each and every woman without interruption. Now and then he fell to the floor. Then they would trample him. When the police finally arrived, his face was beyond recognition. Having taken him for the victim, they asked him: Whom do you accuse?

Madame C... (She was the lady of the house.)

Do you have any witnesses?

Alas, said he, she killed them all. Go have a look, they're lying behind the armchairs.

Well, that's a rotten stroke of luck, they said. To have had so many witnesses and to lose them straight off.

So they took Plume away to the hospital. There were no vacancies. So they took him to another one. A military hospital.

Another one of these fellows with facial wounds, shouted the doctor in charge. Who, just because his nose has been knocked sideways, thinks he can be declared unfit for service. My lad, tomorrow at five o'clock in the morning you will be on your way. He turned to the nurse and said: Take this down. He's part of the convoy leaving for the front tomorrow. Next!

Mme C..., who wanted to display her zeal, was the nurse on duty that night at the hospital. Plume saw her in the nick of time.

One of us, he said, is going to undergo a very rough quarter of an hour. May heaven help me just this one time. Having slipped into the pharmacy, he grabbed a jar containing a good liter and a half of tincture of iodine and having brutally gagged Mme C... with his handkerchief, he proceeded to pour the mixture all over her head and face (the liquid seeping into her mouth and onto her tongue through the handkerchief stiffened her up like a board). He also poured the tincture into her ears and eyes. The latter he pried open by force.

It stings a bit, he said. But it does the job magnificently. Come now, don't be a sissy. This product is recommended by doctors everywhere.

The tincture continued to seep in. When the ghastly mummy's head was discovered the following day, the criminal was already long gone, lying dead on a road on the northern front, his belly torn open by a mortar shell, a strange smile on his face, that same sad yet serene smile he had often flashed while still alive.

Translated by Richard Sieburth • French | France

Deuxième mort de Plume

Plume, en sortant le matin, constata que la ville était complètement déserte.

...Ils auraient quand même pu m'avertir! pensa-t-il et il se mit à errer dans la ville.

Enfin il aperçut un agent; plus loin il y en avait encore un. Aux grands carrefours était resté un agent... Ça, c'est bien la race germanique...pensa-t-il et il se remit à errer dans la ville.

Il en aborda un et lui demanda l'adresse du *Haydn-Museum*, espérant que l'autre s'empresserait de le mettre au courant de tout. L'agent indiqua le chemin, puis salua. Plume s'adressa à un autre, qui lui repondit de même. Au fond, ils détestent les étrangers, pensait A., et il recommença d'errer dans la ville.

Le temps passait. Il se mit à pleuvoir.

Demain, se dit-il, j'irai voir les musée et arrangerai un peu les tableaux à mon goût, car, comme ils sont là disposés, je ne m'y intéresse pas beaucoup.

Le lendemain, il était donc occupé à décrocher des toiles quand les troupes et puis les habitants rentrèrent en ville.

"Vous auriez quand même pu nous prévenir, lui dirent ceux-ci; avoir été pourrir toute une nuit dehors, en pleine pluie avec femme et enfants, il ne faut pas demander, avec les pneumonies qui vont suivre inévitablement, et le désarroi général, tous les frais que ça va nous occasionner.

Mais, dit-il, je vous ai avertis. Je vous ai envoyé une lettre hier.

— "Ah!" et ils sent vont à la *Hauptpost*. On trouve la lettre.

"Bien, dit le chef de la police, vous pouvez aller."

Plume sort. Puis, au coin de la rue, il a peur. Il s'enfuit à toutes jambes. Trop tard. Deux coups de feu retentissent. L'espion a vécu.

Second Death of Plume

Sallying forth one morning, Plume noticed that the city was completely deserted.

...They could have given me some sort of warning, he thought, as he proceeded to wander about the city.

Finally he caught sight of a policeman; there was another one farther along. Policemen were stationed at all the major intersections... How typical of the German race...he thought, as he went on wandering about the city.

He approached a policeman and asked for directions to the *Haydn-Museum*, hoping that the officer would will fill him in on what was happening. Having provided him with the directions, the officer proceeded to salute. Plume addressed himself to another one, who replied in similar fashion. Basically they detest foreigners, A. thought, and went on wandering about the city.

Time was passing. It was starting to rain.

Tomorrow, he said to himself, I'll go visit the museums and rearrange the pictures a bit to suit my taste, for the way they have been hung does little to arouse my interest.

The following day he was therefore busy removing the paintings when the troops reentered the city, followed by the local citizenry.

You could have given us some sort of warning, the citizens said to him. Having had to spend the whole night rotting outdoors with our children and wives in the driving rain, exposed to the pneumonias that will inevitably ensue and prey to the general disarray, no question but that this is going to cost us a pretty penny.

But I did warn you, he said, I sent you a letter yesterday.

Really? And off they go to the *Hauptpost*. The letter is found.

Fine, said the police chief, You're now free to go.

Plume leaves. Then, at the corner of the street, he takes fright. He speeds off as fast as his legs can take him. Too late. Two shots ring out. The spy survived.

JOKHA AL-HARTHI is an academic and a novelist from Oman. An assistant professor at Sultan Qaboos University, she has published ten books including collections of short stories, novels, and children's books. Her recent novel *Narinjah* (Bitter Orange) won the Sultan Qaboos Award for Culture, Arts, and Literature in 2016.

وردة ميمونة

لما وِلِدَتْ ميمونة لم يكن في تجعيدة جسدها الخارج للتو من الرحم أي شيء غريب، سوى وحمة سخيفة أسفل قدمها اليمنى، ولكن أمها، التي بدأت بالتفكير فيما ينبغي عمل بعد الولادة، قالت ساهمة: "فيها شيء غريب". في يومها السابع ذبح أبو ميمونة شاة وتصدق بوزن شعرها المحلوق فضة، واختفت التجاعيد من جسد ميمونة وظلت الوحمة.

لما انقضت أربعون النفاس، وانفضت الزائرات، وطُويَت البسط الجديدة والسجاجيد، ورُفِعَت صواني التمر والفاكهة، تعرفت أم ميمونة الغريب في مولودتها: نظرة عينيها.

تفرست فيها مرارا وهي تستحضر وجوه إخوتها في أقطمتهم: خالد وجهه مثل العلكة الممضوغة، ومحمود وجهه مدور مثل البدر، نفثت في صدرها وتمتمت كأن محمودا مازال بين يديها: "يخزي العين"، ووجه سليمان كان مليئا بحبوب الحساسية، فكرت الأم إن المسكين مازال يعاني منها، أما هلال فوُلد بوجه مسحوب إلى ذقنه، لكن أهدابه الطويلة أضفت عليه جاذبية خاصة، تشوشت أفكار الأم، لم ينظر أي من أولادها الرضع إليها هذه النظرة، هذه النظرة الغريبة التي لا تستطيع فهمها.

استشارت أم ميمونة جارتها أم عبدالرحمن، التي لم تَر ما تتحدث عنه الأم، بل بدت لها المولودة مثل ابنتها عائشة تماما، ولكنها أرادت تطييب خاطرها فوعدتها أن تكلم أخاها الشيخ سعود ليكتب للرضيعة حجابا. زُمَّ الحجاب بخيط أسود في رقبة ميمونة، وحرصت الأم على تقميطها أمام الجارات لئلا يرى الحجاب أحد، ولكن نظرة الرضيعة الغريبة بقيت، فتحولت حيرة الأم إلى قلق. . . . .

Translated by
MARILYN BOOTH

Maimouna's Rose

When Maimouna emerged from her mother's womb, her wrinkled little body seemed perfectly ordinary, except for a silly little birthmark on the bottom of her right foot. Though her mother's mind was occupied with remembering all that she had to do now that the baby was born, she did say to herself, "There's something strange about the girl." But she was too distracted to give it any thought. On her seventh day, Maimouna's father had a sheep slaughtered in her honor and its meat distributed. He gave alms as well, silver equal to the weight of the hair that had been shaved from the infant's head. The wrinkles on Maimouna's body slowly disappeared. The birthmark stayed.

It was only when Umm Maimouna's forty-day recovery period was over, and the stream of visiting women had dwindled, and the new carpets had been rolled up and the date-and-fruit trays put away, that she realized what it was about her tiny daughter that was so strange. It was her gaze.

As soon as it struck her, she began studying Maimouna's face, looking at her time and time again. As she did so she recalled the baby faces of her other children peeping out from their swaddling blankets. Khalid's face had looked like a wad of well-chewed gum, while Mahmoud's had been as round and full as the moon. At that memory, she expelled a little puff of air in the direction of the baby's chest and muttered, just as if Mahmoud were still cradled in her arms, Spite the evil eye! Sulayman's face had been covered in pimples. The poor thing still suffered from skin allergies, his mother sighed. And then there was Hilal, his face long and thin and hollow, but with lush eyelashes that gave him special appeal. But her thoughts were troubled. As nursing infants, none of her other children had ever given her a look like this—such a strange stare, one that she couldn't understand at all.

Umm Maimouna sought the advice of Umm Abd al-Rahman, her neighbor, who could not even see what the mother was talking about. She thought the baby was the spitting image of her own gorgeous little Aisha. Wanting to put the woman's mind at ease, though, she promised to speak to her brother. Shaykh Saud could write out a charm to protect the child. The amulet was fastened around Maimouna's neck with a black thread, and her mother carefully tucked it into her swaddling whenever the neighbors were around, lest someone notice it. But the baby's peculiar steady gaze did not go away and her mother's puzzlement turned to anxiety.

Maimouna's arms and legs grew, and her wholesomely brown face was rounding out. She batted the air with her hands and kicked her little feet upward, and now and then she let out a series of cooing and babbling sounds. But her mother took no delight in any of it, preoccupied as she was with monitoring the strange look in her child's eyes, which seemed never to vary.

Their home was fourth in the row of houses just to the right of the mosque, facing Salem's shop, the barbershop, and the bakery where bread was kneaded, shaped, and baked every day by hand. The house's wooden front door with its carvings led, as did the doors to all of the other houses, into a roomy courtyard lined with lemon trees and quince and rose bushes. A single palm tree stooped over the little canal as if to slake its thirst in the water flowing just beneath its branches. The canal was roofed and walled in by a wooden structure, sheltering the mother as she bathed. And then it would shield her daughter Maimouna as the baby grew into a girl. The structure supported the doddering palm tree, too, so ancient that it had long since ceased to produce any dates.

On that day, as the mother immersed herself in the stream of water for the ritual cleansing that would end her forty-day *nifas*, she made a decision. This really would be her last child. She tipped the bucket of water over her head, once, twice, again, and scrubbed her body with a rough loofah, wary of pressing her breasts hard enough that her milk would ooze out. Trying to avoid remembering how frightening the recent birth had been, she concentrated on the thought that it would be the last time. Yes, she murmured to herself, the last time that the women would say to her, So, did you get a taste of sweet pain, dearie? Yes, indeed, she had tasted it many times! And she had truly seen "stars at noon and the remote, invisible mountains on the Isle of Masira," as a woman would say after a hard and painful birth. Ever since her first pregnancy, those women had kept repeating the same thing, reminding her that she would go through it all again, in every childbirth. Sweet pain, my stars—enough! Enduring such pain time and again did not mean you ever got used to such torment, and then for women to mock the awfulness of it by calling it "sweet" didn't make it any less awful. And now here she was blessed with the girl she had waited for, the fulfillment of her dreams after four boys. What more could she want? This is more than enough, she murmured. This is our blessing, our gift. But then she hesitated; must she now say, as she bathed off the remnants of her afterbirth, *praise be to God*? Was it appropriate to say such a thing when she was washing her body? Or ought she to keep the Almighty's name unblemished, by not mentioning it at such a moment, in such circumstances? She squeezed the water from her long hair, section by section, trying to keep at bay her awareness that in the past, after every childbirth, she had promised herself that this would be the last one. But then she would forget, and grow eager and expectant, and so there would come another baby.

On that day, she had finished her ablutions and was getting ready to leave the *falaj* when a sudden flash of light on the water surprised her. The sunshine coming through the cracks in the wooden roof shot its reflection into the water so strongly that the light dazed her. It seemed to pierce right through, and then she could see into the depths as clear as day. This was the moment when, all of a sudden, it was revealed: the source of the strangeness she had sensed but not understood ever since her daughter's birth forty days before. She had given her head such a shake that her damp, squeezed hair had come undone. It is the look in her eyes! This girl looks at me strangely. Yes, the look in this baby girl's eyes is nothing like anything I've ever seen on the face of any other newborn.

She picked up her folded clothes from the stone lip of the falaj and

Translated by Marilyn Booth • Arabic | Oman

put them on, dabbed a bit of Indian aloe oil behind each ear, and left the canal, heading toward the room that opened onto the courtyard by means of Arabian-style arches and columns. She heard the faint cry of her baby and went into the middle room, which held the little cradle and the pallet on which the mother slept. None of the others had cried this way, she thought. Their crying had been sharp and unending, but this little girl's was a faint, punctuated sobbing. She picked up the little bundle and gave the baby her breasts. The girl opened her eyes and looked full into her mother's eyes. The woman shivered and remembered the gleaming light on the canal and the strange gaze revealed in the depths. It was as though the girl's eyes held a secret that could only well up from the canal waters themselves. Her mouth was sipping at the milk, not sucking it hard. The mother sensed drops of water on her back. Was she sweating on this winter day, or was it dripping from her still-damp hair? In that moment she brought back to mind the faces of her children when they were as many days old as Maimouna was now. She remembered their screaming and the way they had nursed, fixed onto her breast, determined not to let it escape. She remembered their eyes, never fixed on anything. It was when all of these images passed through her head, as she studied her baby daughter, that she had decided to seek the advice of Umm Abd al-Rahman.

> By the time she turned six, she was no longer making any sounds at all. Her eyes seemed ever wider, enlarged by that peculiar look.

Despite the neighbor's advice and help, despite the amulet she had procured that Maimouna's mother fixed around the baby's neck with a black thread, and despite Maimouna's steady growth (even with such finicky nursing), Maimouna's gaze didn't change. Nor did the faint sounds she made grow louder as her body grew bigger. Instead, they became less frequent and more hushed, day after day and year after year. By the time she turned six, she was no longer making any sounds at all. Her eyes seemed ever wider, enlarged by that peculiar look.

Her mother did hold fast to the decision she had made on the day she had cleansed herself fully of Maimouna's birth. She had no more children. She paid no attention to the urgings of her husband, nor to the hints she heard from her neighbors about the danger she was putting herself in. He would take another wife, they insinuated. She persisted in refusing to have any more than these five children, and she was adamant about forbidding him the delights of this mundane life although he was only in his early forties. Five healthy babies, and praise the Lord! she said to him, and to the neighbors. A blessed gift from the Lord of Heaven and Earth, boys I can rely on and a girl who'll take care of me in my old age. God preserve them all.

Maimouna's husband did not take another wife. She was his cousin, and he loved her fragrance and the heat of her embrace. He loved to hear her laughing at dawn. Besides, he did not want to bear the responsibility for maintaining two homes. And in the end he was persuaded by what she said about the children. But he did not discover the secret of her wound.

No, as deep inside of her as that wound went, her husband did not uncover its secret. Cleansing herself for that last time, she had believed that making this decision to stop having children would help her to forget the pains of it, this time as she had before. A year later, or maybe two, and no doubt she would fill the house all over again, once another two or three children arrived. But the mystery of her newborn daughter's stare revealed something to her, a flash of something, as though it was a sunbeam slicing the canal, and yet as steady and unchanging as only the deepest waters can be.

The mother had always longed to give birth to a girl even if she had hidden this hope of hers carefully from her cousin. She shared his joy as one boy after another came. She even felt complacently grateful for the envy of the women in the neighborhood as they witnessed her surrounded by young lions who would spare her the toil of thinking about the vicissitudes of the future. But her fancies about a little girl had grown and swelled inside her, even as—every time she washed the afterbirth away at the falaj—she swore yet again that this was the last time. But then the longings would accumulate inside her, forming a knot of annoyance at herself for having made such a vow. She would break it; she must. What was the worth of a mother who had no daughter to resemble her? No daughter whose hair she could braid, no little girl to be proud of. Would her boys bathe her when she grew old and infirm? Would they gossip with her, sharing sharp and mocking observations about the women of the quarter? Would they bake bread and cook rice for her? Would they weep with her when her animals died or her husband grew ill? She had to have a daughter, a girl who would be just like her.

Translated by Marilyn Booth • Arabic | Oman

But Maimouna, brown-skinned and slender and silent, was as unlike her mother as could be. She grew as tall and angular as a spear; and like a spear, she could stab mercilessly at the dreams her mother cherished. When her mother finally spanked her for the first time, the woman was screaming at her in desperation. Why are you looking at me like that? Huh? What's wrong with you? What's it about me to make you stare at me like that? Are you an idiot or what? At her words, the canal-water sparkle in her daughter's eyes went out. The girl clamped her eyes shut like the lid of a little chest snapping closed. After that, her eyes seemed to look only inward. In her mother's presence she opened them only rarely.

Maimouna is a little different. That was all that her father said. Her brothers tried to draw their sister into their rough play, but she wouldn't respond, except when it came to the spinning game. Whoever could whirl the fastest without falling down was the winner. Maimouna was not the fastest, but she never fell down. Her brothers took no notice of her oddly silent ways. They dragged her along to school, where she failed the first grade, and to Salem's shop where she took a liking to one particular kind of sweet, a lollipop with colorful swirly spirals. The neighbors' son, Abd al-Rahman, bought her one every time he saw her outside the door of their house, which faced the shop directly. In the summer her brothers took her to the farms and collected hard unripe dates for her and fed her on green mangoes with salt. They squeezed little lemons onto green bananas and stuffed them into her mouth. They made her sit down on a tree stump to watch them as they tried to outdo each other at killing frogs. They rubbed hard at the birthmark on the sole of her foot with palm fronds, threw her into the water, and dried her off by swinging her back and forth vigorously between them. One would grab her hands and the other would hold onto her feet and they would swing her hard into the air, screaming, Today's catch, who will buy it? Fresh catch, who will buy it? They would carry her back to the house, her *dishdasha*—now dry—fluttering like a banner across the nape of Mahmoud's neck.

But Maimouna's brothers forgot all of their amusing pranks and games when, ten years later, the scandal broke. Mahmoud's face went dark with shame, and Sulayman's face broke out in a rash. Hilal paced the house, bellowing, and Khalid left his wife in the birthing room when he heard the news.

Maimouna was nine years old when the rose slid down the wall for the first time. She was standing beside the old palm tree, facing it and staring at a point somewhere near its crown. She was lost in thought, oblivious to the three birds Hilal had targeted with his arrows, and which he would grill for her when their father stepped out to perform his late-afternoon prayers. Her mother was lashing her with loud and disapproving words. Are you waiting for a revelation? Has the Angel Gabriel not come down to earth yet?

It was a clear and quiet late afternoon. The sounds of noisy chatter in front of the barbershop had died down, and the boys had tired of shattering their Pepsi bottles in front of Salem's shop. Her brothers were trying to look as though they were engrossed in their schoolwork. Soon their father would be back from the mosque and then he would drink his coffee and stretch out his legs on the mat in the shade of the quince bush. At that moment, as soon as the mother had stopped shouting, the instant she finished her sentence, the rose slid down, a rose infused with a deep and vivid pink. It slid gently over the low wall of the courtyard and landed safely on the ground as if a hand had placed it carefully just at Maimouna's feet.

On the day the scandal loomed, everyone was busy. The mother had spent the whole day at Umm Abd al-Rahman's house, standing in front of the vats of meat, weighing out all the rice, urging the other neighborhood women to hurry with slicing the onions and tomatoes and browning the almonds and raisins. She and Umm Abd al-Rahman unrolled the new red carpets and lined up the bottles of scent and went around the whole house swinging their incense burners. When the sun set and she came home, she barely had time to dip her body into the canal and put on her embroidered gown, gold bracelets, and the heavy necklace that she had inherited from her mother.

The rose fell onto the ground, and Maimouna's right foot moved slightly so that one of the rose petals brushed her sole. Her braids swung as she lowered her face to the ground. When the petal touched her birthmark the sparkle of a sunbeam on the water lit up her eyes for just a flash. She sensed sweet water trickle down her throat. She raised her head. She hadn't picked up the rose. She had simply stared at it.

Two days later, a rose slid to the ground again. Maimouna was standing motionless in the courtyard, staring at the wall. Her father was still at the mosque, and her mother was making the afternoon coffee. The rose dropped

Translated by Marilyn Booth • Arabic | Oman

from over the wall and came quietly down. Its soft edges brushed the wall brick by brick as it dropped, while two or three petals wafted away from it and landed upside down just steps from Maimouna. She picked up the rose by its slender green stem and brought it close to her eyes. She flattened the soft stem between her fingers, but the flower's yellow corolla remained brightly visible.

A week later Maimouna walked slowly to the rosebush. One of her brothers had overwatered the trees, and the soil around them was still sticky to her feet. She pulled off the biggest rose, interlaced her fingers, and closed her palms, making a little cage for the rose. She passed along by the palm tree that leaned against the roofing over the canal and stopped. The January gusts pummeled her clothes. Her mother, mounting the two or three steps from the courtyard to the reception room where she would sort the dates, shouted, Come inside, Maimouna, put on a warm woollen sweater, the air is cold. Come on! But Maimouna didn't budge. She waited a few moments. The rose slid down from the neighbors' house, and all at once Maimouna raised her arms and threw her rose over the wall. She stood there for a moment staring at her empty hands then bent over to pick up the rose on the ground in front of her. She plunged it into the water where it sat, a few petals detaching to float away with the current. When their father came home he led Maimouna, her eyes closed, from where she stood at the stone lining to the falaj into the main room of the house. Her mother wrapped her in her woollen sweater. The girl opened her eyes and stared at her mother, who sighed deeply and tossed her a date. That night, the mother stroked Maimouna's soft hair, and the rare, special look came back into her eyes. My poor girl, she whispered. Such little luck you've had. But anyway, praise God, praise God.

When the mother had made certain that her gold necklace would be visible behind the translucent weave of her head veil, she put her hennaed feet into the gilt flowery slippers and went off to the wedding. Yesterday, her sons had contributed to the neighborhood barber's daily profits, and then they had taken the bridegroom to the city barber who used a twisted thread to pluck out the stray hairs around the groom's moustache. For a customer like Abd al-Rahman who was coming to him as part of his wedding festivities, accompanied by his friends, the barber reserved a special facial treatment using steam, and washed his hair with fancy shampoo and balsam conditioner. He joined in as they teased the groom, making suggestive remarks and winking into his face. The young men cheered and whistled as they brought Abd al-Rahman back to the village where he would complete his ritual bathing.

Mahmoud was flustered, trying to conceal his phone while texting the neighbors' daughter Aisha. *Here they are going first, and we'll be the next.* Aisha had taken great care to appear at her very best, wanting her neighbor to notice how superbly turned out and carefully groomed she was, this neighbor who would soon visit their home to engage her for her son, once Mahmoud graduated, later in the year, and approached his family with his wishes. Aisha had put on face powder and outlined her eyes in kohl. She was thinking hard about how to respond to Mahmoud's message in the most elegant way possible. Uncertain, she turned over the phone in her hands. He had given it to her two weeks before, and she had hidden it under her clothes in the wardrobe. She always kept it in silent mode fearing its discovery by her mother or father or—God forbid!—her proud and jealous brother Abd al-Rahman.

At the very end of their row of houses sat the bridegroom's house, and there, strong words were passing between Umm Abd al-Rahman and the bride's mother. The bride was the daughter of Salim the shop owner, and she was the prettiest and the most well-turned-out girl in the village. The other women tried to intervene between the two mothers, wanting to calm them down. They tried to persuade the bridegroom's mother that it really was the custom these days for the bride to delay making an appearance until nearly midnight. Umm Abd al-Rahman threw her arm around her neighbor's shoulder and said, Help me pass the trays to everyone. Once she could bring her face closer to her neighbor's, she whispered, This is the least of it. Imagine, her sisters took her to Muscat as if no one here is capable of doing her up properly, and then her mother is rude to me. What am I going to say to Abu Abd al-Rahman when he comes with the men to celebrate his son's wedding? Shall I say, This missy bride hasn't even arrived yet? Aisha will take care of telling him. Uhh, I don't see Aisha—where has she disappeared to? Maybe she went off to bring Maimouna? In fact, Maimouna's mother had not thought to wonder where Maimouna was, but if Aisha didn't lead her out to watch the wedding, it was likely that the girl would remain in her room, sitting still and silent as a stone. That's the way she behaved most of

Translated by Marilyn Booth • Arabic | Oman

the time these days, as though she were gradually turning into some mere thing whom no one ever saw or heard.

After the marriage contract had been officially accepted and witnessed, the men lingered in the mosque. They had their coffee and sweets and were chatting about this and that. Abd al-Rahman would glance at his watch, and then at his phone, waiting for a call from his sister Aisha telling him the bride had arrived. But his sister's call signal arrived elsewhere. Mahmoud's phone lit up and he got to his feet, making the excuse that he was going to fetch more coffee. He held his breath as he read. *Since that first rose, when you sent it sliding over the wall to me, responding to my rose, I've known that our wedding day must come sooner or later.* Mahmoud shook his head. Rose? Roses? *Wurud wa-rudud*? What roses? What responses? Who is sliding a rose at her across the wall? This Aisha is very romantic, full of imagination. Girls! So, should he bring her roses, or what? He still couldn't believe that finally, they had actually had a real conversation, after all the surreptitious glances and smiles. And then he couldn't believe it when she accepted his phone as a gift. How surprising girls could be! Roses? Whatever you say, Sitt Aisha. Beauty deserves roses.

With the bride's arrival, as she was ushered to the raised settee in the front room, Aisha phoned her brother. It was not long before the file of men arrived and seated Abd al-Rahman at his bride's side. The singing and dancing started immediately. Guests tossed jasmine petals at the pair. Abd al-Rahman gave his sister a little kick to let her know that it was time. She announced that the wedding feast awaited their guests. She took her brother's arm as the sister of the bride took the bride's arm. The mother trilled in congratulations and preceded them to open the door into the bedroom. She was surprised to find the doorknob broken, but she hid her chagrin and kept her back to the door so that the womenfolk of the bride's family would not notice. She shoved the door open with her body to let the bridal pair inside.

The mother flung away her fruit knife and dashed toward the sounds of people screaming out her daughter's name. Maimouna!

Abd al-Rahman was the first to react. At his loud gasp, Maimouna turned toward him and opened her eyes to their widest, staring into his. He let out another sound, something between a gasp and a moan, and nearly slid to the ground, but he managed to stay upright by leaning back against the wardrobe. Cries went up all around as Abd al-Rahman was imprisoned behind the bodies pushing forward through the doorway. Maimouna, her eyes closed now, writhed on the bed, naked except for an undershirt that reached only as far as the top of her thighs. The mother flung away her fruit knife and dashed toward the sounds of people screaming out her daughter's name. Maimouna! She saw her daughter's thin form, all but naked, and twisting on the bridal bed, her saliva dampening the sheets and her fingernails scratching the stuffing from the pillows. The mother screamed and fell onto her daughter, but Maimouna resisted her grasp ferociously, aiming her fingers straight at her mother's eyes. Her mother had no choice but to retreat. When Umm Abd al-Rahman and Aisha tried to drag her from the bed she scratched their faces, and she bit every hand that came near her until it bled. Blood mingled with clods of dried mud that had clung to her feet, and it spattered across the bed. From her mouth flew wads of paper. Whenever anyone tried to come near she clung more tightly to the bedposts and her raspy breathing grew louder and faster. The mother fell to the floor. Women hurried to tell the men, but some of them blockaded the doorway to prevent anyone from coming inside. The girl was naked, after all.

Abd al-Rahman, though paralyzed by the scene in front of him, suddenly noticed the shreds of paper Maimouna was chewing on and spitting out. He could tell where they had come from; he knew the book she had torn the pages from. He had given it to her two years before, on her fifteenth birthday. She always seemed transfixed by the rose bushes outside. He had thought that this book, with its lushly colored illustrations of all kinds of flowers, would make her happy. She was such a calm and quiet girl. She smiled at him every time he saw her hovering in front of the doorway. She never refused the sweets that, now and then, he bought for her. Aisha sometimes brought her home, and he didn't remember ever hearing her shout or speak hoarsely or even breathe hard. This was another creature entirely. Had she suddenly been possessed by the jinn? He shouted at the frightened women. Bring someone to read the Qur'an over her. And leave the room, all of you, leave the room. Now.

When her brother Mahmoud rushed into the room Maimouna was clinging to the bed with both hands and both legs. Though her chest was pressed

Translated by Marilyn Booth • Arabic | Oman

close against the scored pillows, her body was heaving and vibrating almost as though she were dancing. She was completely covered in sweat and saliva, and the rattling in her throat had turned into a thin and grievous wail. Mahmoud pulled her away from the bed, though it required all the strength he had. He wrapped her in an enormous shawl that one of the women had handed to him. He threw her across his shoulders as though she were a roll of rags. He strode through the crowd of people. His sister hung lifelessly across the damp nape of his neck, as Mahmoud brought her home.

Born in 1980 in Algiers, **SAMIRA NEGROUCHE** trained as a physician before concentrating on poetry. Her work engages with aesthetic and physical borders, and she has collaborated with several visual artists and musicians. Her books include *Le Jazz des oliviers* and *Six arbres de fortune autour de ma baignoire*.

Nœuds en zigzag

Fenêtre de rien: plane

ainsi parle le vieux chêne
qui du bas de son demi mètre carré
fume
ce n'est pas de la moquette étranger
mais de la planche épongée
absorbée et remâchée
abord lisse non ne lisse pas tes yeux
sur le carré exponentiel circule
il n'y a rien à signaler
d'où que tu viennes
le sentier ne mène nulle part
ne te hâte pas à l'abordage

Zigzag
Knots

Window on nothing: glide

thus spoke the old oak

who from the bottom of his half-a-square-meter

smokes up

not the carpet, stranger,

but a booze-soaked board

absorbed, chewed over

smooth manner no don't smooth down your eyes

on the exponential square, keep moving

nothing here to see

wherever you come from

the path leads nowhere

don't rush to the attack

Poussière d'alcôve: tourne

qu'importe si tu presses le pas
sous l'arche centrale
que tu insinues ton ombre furtive
dans le tronc du lampadaire
la porte qui mène mène
au vieux chêne

Fenêtre d'oubli: refrain

mon frère à la manche délavée
sous la lumière hésitante
lève ses doigts de charbon
son verre rayé
ainsi va le vieux chêne
à rythmer le monologue
des naufragés
blouse de docker
ou chemise thaï taillée à la mesure
c'est à cette enseigne
sans adresse
qu'accourent les souliers
et toi l'ami—veille

Ciel: en coupole

ici est né un chant
où la corde est soumise
sa brise circulaire
redresse les voiles

Dust of the bedchamber: turn

it makes no difference if you hurry
under the central archway
or insinuate your furtive shadow
into the streetlight's trunk
the door that opens opens
on the old oak

Window of forgetting: refrain

my brother with faded shirtsleeves
under the hesitant light
raises his coal fingers
his striped glass
and the old oak goes on
syncopating monologues
of the shipwrecked,
stevedore's overalls
or custom-tailored Thai shirt
it's to his shop-sign
with no street address
that the shoes come running
and you, friend—keep watch

Sky: under the dome

here a song is born
where the strings submit
its circular breeze
raises the sails

Translated by Marilyn Hacker • French | Algeria

Fenêtre: horizon

on y entre par la mer

chuchote le vieux chêne

et ceux qu'on y croise

soutiennent les yeux

on y entre par la mer

le blanc aveugle le bleu

et le bleu irrigue

on n'y accoste pas l'ami

la barque est déjà à quai

hâte-toi vers les hautes herbes

que t'aveugle le soleil

que te prenne la colline

Vagues: vagues

on y entre par les collines

des ravins y ruissellent

entre ses jambes dit la légende

et des femmes sauvages

s'inventent

on y entre par un fer forgé

enroulé avec adresse

par des mains ici nées

ou réfugiées

on y entre par la rue de Tanger

par un crissement humide

par des débris en collision

et par les courbes qu'on

devine.

Window: horizon

you enter by sea
whispers the old oak
and those whose path you cross
hold your gaze
you enter by sea
the white blinds the blue
and the blue irrigates
you don't greet the friend
the boat is already by the quay
rush toward the high grass
let the sun blind you
let the hill take you

Waves: waves

you enter from the hills
ravines flow there
between your legs says the legend
and savage women
invent themselves
you enter through iron filigrees
adroitly wrought
by native hands
or refugees'
you enter from the rue Tanger
by a humid rustling
by fragments in collision
and by the curves you
guess at

Translated by Marilyn Hacker • French | Algeria

Fenêtre du dedans: relief

hâte-toi l'ami

d'apporter ta mesure

ici est né un chant

pour ceux qui se souviennent

ici est né l'oubli de ceux

qui abordent

de ceux qui reviennent

par des portes inconnues

des sentiers non conquis

presse-toi étranger

la vague est atteinte

ici est la mesure

on y entre par la mer.

Indoor window: in depth

hurry, friend
bring your measure
a song is born here
for those who remember
here the ones who dock
beside you are forgotten
the ones who return
by unknown doors
unmastered pathways
hurry, stranger
the wave was mounted
here is the measure
you enter by sea

Translated by Marilyn Hacker • French | Algeria

Born in East Berlin in 1951, KATJA
LANGE-MÜLLER is one of the most
idiosyncratic and respected authors
writing in German today. Her novellas,
short stories, and novels are consistently
experimental, blending autobiographical
elements with anecdotes and critical
observation in sinuous sentences that
"envelop" the reader.

Verfrühte Tierliebe

Teil I: Käfer

Seit ich die Tiere kenne,
liebe ich die Pflanzen.
—H. Beyer, Schauspieler

Unsere Schule war ein fast quadratischer Bau aus rotgelben Ziegeln, unter
dessen Dach früher einmal eine Schokoladenfabrikation gehaust haben soll,
was ich manchmal für möglich hielt, wegen des vanilleähnlichen Geruchs,
der—schwach, doch penetrant genug in seiner Andersartigkeit—den übli-
chen Bohnerwachs-Pisse-Gestank durchdrang, wenn es sehr heiß wurde von
der Sonne im Sommer oder, schon seltener, im Winter von den gußeisernen
Heizkörpern, deren abblätternde braune Rostschutzfarbpartikel ich eine
Zeitlang sammelte, wie auch von den specksteinernen Fensterbänken die
krepierten Fliegen, die ich, am liebsten während der Mathematikstunden . . .

A Precocious Love of Animals

Part I: Beetles

> *Ever since I discovered animals*
> *I have loved plants.*
> —H. Beyer, actor

Our school was a near-square russet brick building, which had reportedly once housed a chocolate factory, something I occasionally thought might be true when a whiff of vanilla—weak, yet sufficiently pungent in its strangeness—penetrated the habitual stench of beeswax and piss in the heat of the summer sun or, more rarely, in winter, by the heat of the cast-iron radiators, particles of whose peeling brown anti-rust paint I collected for a while, as I did the flies that had croaked on the soapstone window seats, which I would dismember with my mother's hair-removal tweezers while hiding behind a wobbly tower of textbooks, preferably during math lessons, into their component parts, before heaping these—the bodies with the bodies, the heads with the heads, the legs with the legs, the wings with the wings—into four different-colored *Sprachlos* cigarillo boxes.

Like a small lidless box inside a larger one perforated with square glazed air holes and peepholes, the playground lay inside the school, and across it scampered two rats, not especially fast or close together, throughout the autumn of my sixth grade, always early in the day, before assembly, until one morning the caretaker knocked at least one of the two dead with his coal shovel. The other, however, far from running away in panic, pattered in a tight circle around the victim, as if it were drunk, shocked, and confused, and such was the caretaker's surprise that he kneeled down in spite of his rheumatoid arthritis to take a closer look at the remaining rat, still clutching the shovel for safety's sake. Unable to believe his eyes, even at this close range, or fearing for their sight (on account of the rat), he reached for the reading glasses that were otherwise tucked, solely for decorative purposes, along with an old fountain pen, into the bib of his never-truly-clean, yet always stiffly starched and perfectly pressed overalls.

Having gone to such lengths, the caretaker could not fail to notice that the surviving rat's eyeballs were completely milky, and that it grasped between the yellow fangs of its mouth, fringed with bristling, quivering whiskers, a twig by which—to quote the caretaker—its "fallen fellow rodent" had led it "through life like a faithful guide dog."

Until the caretaker took permanent retirement around the end of the new-year holidays, Rolf—for that, he told us, was what he had christened the white-eyed rat, with the aid of some Pilsner lager, "in memory of the dead"—lived in the caretaker's boiler room, where the rat was nice and warm; and so were we on the rare occasions we were allowed to feed it—but only with bits of bread, never with sausage.

Almost exactly in the middle of the virtually rectangular playground stood—I do not wish to say "grew," for compared to what I imagine "growing" to mean, that which was taking place was happening, if indeed it was still happening at all, at an almost imperceptibly slow rate—a forty-foot pedunculate oak tree. The fact that we were even aware that this was a pedunculate oak was the apparently logical result of our old biology teacher's claim that, in the absence of any other or further clues, one could identify a tree purely by its bark structure. On not one spring day of a single year of our decade-long acquaintance was the tree to be seen anything other than bare. Each and every fresh shoot that tried to break out of the oak every twelve months vanished like a mirage as soon as this process so much as tinged the outermost tips of its many-forked branches; golden-ass caterpillars would gobble up the buds, immediately and utterly.

> *Maybe they were discovered by a wretched worm of a man called Goldenass, but there was not the slightest evidence that this was the origin of their name, and thus to this day I have no idea why these creatures are called golden-ass caterpillars.*

Maybe they were discovered by a wretched worm of a man called Goldenass, but there was not the slightest evidence that this was the origin of their name, and thus to this day I have no idea why these creatures are called golden-ass caterpillars. None I have ever seen presents a golden or even a yellow arse, and the threads that emerged from their swollen abdomens as they swung from twig to twig or abseiled earthward were the light gray of spiders' webs. But didn't the tree of which the woody-brown, bristle-tufted golden-ass caterpillar formed the sole buds, shoots, leaves, blossoms, and fruit, go by the equally nonsensical name of "summer oak"?

Sometimes a few perhaps weakened, perhaps clumsy, perhaps escaping golden-ass caterpillars would lie on the ground; they were immediately destroyed, squashed into the gravel with steel toe-caps, stones, and sticks. Otherwise, the golden-ass caterpillars never crossed our minds during our first six years at school, and not even our biology teacher knew of which species of moth they were the preliminary stage. They never pupated; if they did indeed do so—for, after all, they were caterpillars—then it must have been somewhere else, or it lasted just one night, for they would all be gone one morning each time, but whether they too had been devoured by some other creature or had flown out into the world in a changed state, or been atomised—crumbled into dust—remained unfathomable, and so exercised my imagination that in the seventh spring I pulled my grandma's potato knife from my cardigan pocket under my school desk, used it to hollow out a wine cork, stuffed it with the caterpillars I'd picked up in the playground three days previously, and sealed the hole with a lattice of needles. And lo and behold: the first animal-filled prison cork.

At first, my study of the behavior of golden-ass caterpillars under specific architectural and social conditions went off to my relative satisfaction; in the next long break this novel handicraft gained, along with several admirers, a few imitators, and even my test subjects behaved—as they excreted droplets of a bile-green liquid, they tweaked the close-fitting needles incessantly with the pincers of their trophi, squeezed their suckered front feet between them, and pressed their chitinous foreheads to the stainless-steel curtain—exactly as one might expect convicts to behave.

There was only one real problem: I had no idea how I was supposed to feed the golden-ass caterpillars. They had already finished off the one thing I knew they ate—the foliage of the pedunculate oak in our playground. Other trees of the same species probably did exist in our area, in the graveyard perhaps or one of the parks. Yet even if I had sought out and found the nearest pedunculate oak trees, I could safely assume from my accumulated knowledge that they too had been eaten bare by identical golden-ass caterpillars. So I stuffed the leaves of other plants through the bars to the three in the cork, followed by blades of grass, then morsels of apple and turnip. Clearly quite incapable of learning, my golden-ass caterpillars gnawed—though with less than half the belligerence they had first displayed—nothing but the needles, not even one another. Eventually, on the fifth day of the experiment, at about 2:30 in the afternoon, in the middle of a German lesson, just as we were having to write a dictation, they died as if they'd been executed, all at once and virtually simultaneously, their appearance unaltered from the first moment of their imprisonment until that of their death; they were not even any thinner.

ख़ुशियों के गुप्तचर

एक पीली खिड़की इस तरह खुलती है
जैसे खुल रही हों किसी फूल की पंखुड़ियां.

एक चिड़िया पिंजरे की सलाखों को ऐसे कुतरती है
जैसे चुग रही हो अपने ही खेत में धान की बालियां.

मेरे कुछ सपने अब सूख गए हैं
इन दिनों उनसे अलाव जलाता हूं

और जो सपने हरे हैं
उन्हें बटोरकर एक बकरी की भूख मिटाता हूं

मेरी भाषा का सबसे बूढ़ा कवि लाइब्रेरी से लाया है मोटी किताबें
चौराहे पर बैठ सोने की अशर्फ़ियों की तरह बांटता है शब्द

मेरे पड़ोस की बुढ़िया ने ईजाद किया है एक यंत्र जिसमें आंसू डालो, तो
पीने लायक़ पानी अलग हो जाता है, खाने लायक़ नमक अलग.

एक मां इतने ममत्व से देखती है अपनी संतान को
कि उसके दूध की धार से बहने लगती हैं कई नदियां

जो धरती पर बिखरे रक्त के गहरे लाल रंग को
प्रेम के हल्के गुलाबी रंग में बदल देती हैं.

Translated by
ANITA GOPALAN

Secret Agents of Joy

A golden window opens out
Like a petal unfolding in a flower.

A bird nibbles at the bar of her cage
Like pecking in her own farm, a head of grain.

A bunch of my dreams have dried up now
I use them these days to crackle a bonfire

And the dreams that are still tender green
I pick them up to sate a goat's hunger

From the library the oldest poet of my language has borrowed voluminous
    books
Now lounging at a crossroad dispenses words like gold coins

My old woman neighbor has invented a device
From tears she now distils clean potable water, edible salt crystals.

A mother beholds her child with so much love
That from the stream of her milk, several rivers spill forth

Which blanch the deep red color of blood strewn on Earth
Into an innocent pink of love.

Translated by Anita Gopalan • Hindi | India

बायोडाटा

हां, यह बताऊंगा कि क्या-क्या लिखा, कहां-कहां छपा आदि-आदि,
लेकिन यह भी कि एक सिर जहां सारे जंगल सूख गए
और दो आंखें जिनमें भूला हुआ संगीत सितारा बनकर रहता
और एक शरीर जिस पर जगह-जगह ज़ख़्मों के निशान
जैसे पोलिश कवियों ने अपनी कविताएं वहां चिपका दीं.
और एक दिल जिसके होने का अहसास कोलेस्ट्रोल की दवाओं ने कराया
और एक आत्मा जो आवारा बिल्लियों की तरह हमेशा घर से बाहर नज़र आती.

Biodata

Yes, about works written, places published, etc.
But also about a head, where all jungles have shriveled
And two eyes, in which float the stars of the music forgotten
And a body, that is scarred greatly
As if Polish poets have taped their poems all over.
And a heart whose existence the cholesterol pills keep affirming
And a soul that like a stray untamed cat is always seen
In the street outside.

Translated by Anita Gopalan • Hindi | India

मालिक को खुश करने के लिए किसी भी सीमा तक जाने वाला मानवीय दिमाग और अपनी नस्ल का शुरुआती जूता

राजकुमारी महल के बाग में विचर रही थीं कि एक कांटे ने उनके पैरों के साथ गुस्ताखी की और बजाए उसे दंडित करने के राजकुमारी बहुत रोई और बहुत छटपटाई और बड़े जतन से उन्हें पालने वाले राजा पिता तड़प कर रह गए और महल के गलियारों और बाज़ों में खड़े हो धीरे-धीरे बड़ी हो रही राजकुमारी के पैरों से किसी तरह कांटा निकलवाया और हुक्मनामा जारी करवाया कि राज्य में कांटों की गुस्ताखी हद से ज्यादा हो गई है और उन्हें समास करने की मुहिम शुरू कर दी जाए पर योजनाओं के असफल होने और मुहिमों के बांझ रह जाने की शुरुआत के रूप में ढाक बचा और ढाक के तीन पात बचे तो राजा ने आदेश दिया कि सारे राज्य की सड़कों और महल के पूरे हिस्से की जमीन पर फूलों की चादर बिछा दी जाए पर चूंकि फूल बहुत जल्दी मुरझा जाते हैं सो यह भी संभव न हुआ तो राजा ने अपने एक भरोसेमंद मंत्री को इसका इलाज निकालने की जिम्मेवारी दी तो उस मंत्री ने बजाए सारी जमीन पर फूल बिछाने के राजकुमारी के पैरों पर ध्यान जमाया और नर्म कपड़े की कई तहों को चिपका कर मोटी-सी कोई चीज बनाई और राजकुमारी को पहना दी जिसके पार कांटा क्या कांटे का असली बाप भी नहीं पहुंच सकता था और इस तरह एक आदिम जूते का निर्माण हुआ हालांकि जूतेनुमा एक चीज बनाने वाले उस मंत्री किस्म के मानव ने राजकुमारी किस्म की किसी महिला के पैरों को कांटे से बचाने के लिए इलाज ढूंढने से पहले खुद भी कई बार कांटों को भुगता था और दूसरे तमाम लोगों के भी कांटा चुभते देखा था पर नौकर की जमात का वह व्यक्ति मात्र स्वामिभक्ति के पारितोषिक के लिए ही जूता बना पाया।

Human Mind Going to Any Length to Please His Master, and the First Shoe of Its Kind

The princess was taking a stroll in the palace gardens when a thorn took liberty with her feet, and the princess instead of punishing that thorn rather writhed in pain, cried much in pain and her father, the king who had nurtured her painstakingly, was greatly agonized and hanging patiently in the hallways and corridors of the palace somehow got the thorn extracted from the tender feet of his little princess, who had been growing up robustly, after which he issued a decree that since thorns were taking far too many liberties in his kingdom, a campaign program should commence to end this menace but when all plans withered on the vine and only a bare tree with a three-pinnate leaf sticking to it remained, the first signs of the nonsuccess of the plan and the barrenness of the campaign surfaced and then the frustrated king ordered his men to cover all roads of his kingdom and the palace grounds with flowers but since flowers wither very quickly, this plan too did not work and then the king gave the responsibility of finding a solution to his most dependable minister and the minister then instead of sheathing the land with flowers, focused his attention on the princess's feet and folding a soft piece of cloth many times over shaped a thickish cushy thing and made the princess wear it which not even the father of thorns could get past, let alone a tiny little thorn and in this way the first man-made shoe was designed and realized although before finding a solution to protect the feet of a princess-like woman against thorns, that minister kind of human who made a shoe kind of thing had himself suffered thorns several times and seen numerous other people getting thorn pricks but only for a mere reward for his loyalty, that man belonging to the servile class was finally able to make the shoe.

Translated by Anita Gopalan • Hindi | India

दूध के दांत

देह का कपड़ा
देह की गरमी से
देह पर ही सूखता है.
—कृष्णनाथ

मैंने जिन-जिन जगहों पे गाड़े थे अपने दूध के दांत
वहां अब बड़े-खड़े पेड़ लहलहाते हैं.

दूध का सफेद
तनों के कत्थई और पत्तों के हरे में
लौटता है.

जैसे लौटकर आता है कर्मा.
जैसे लौटकर आता है प्रेम.
जैसे विस्मृति में भी लौटकर आती है
कहीं सुनी गई कोई धुन.
बचपन की मासूमियत बुढ़ापे के
सन्निपात में लौटकर आती है.

भीतर किसी खोह में छुपी रहती है
तमाम मौन के बाद भी
लौट आने को तत्पर रहती है हिंसा.

Milk Teeth

Cloth on the body
dries
with the heat of the body
on the body itself.
—Krishna Nath

The places I buried my milk teeth,
tall trees thrive there now.

In the brown of trunk and green of leaves,
the white of milk
returns.

The way our karma returns.
The way our love returns.
The way a tune heard somewhere
returns in the unconscious.
The innocence of childhood
returns in old age, in dementia.

Hiding within, in some cavern
in spite of all the silence
violence is keen to return.

Translated by Anita Gopalan • Hindi | India

लोगों का मन खोलकर देखने की सुविधा मिले
तो हर कोई विश्वासघाती निकले.
सच तो यह है
कि अनुवाद में वफादारी कहीं आसान है.
किसी गूढ़ार्थ के अनुवाद में बेवफाई हो जाए
तो नकचढ़ी कविता नाता नहीं तोड़ लेती.

मेरे भीतर पुरखों जैसी शांति है.
समकालीनों जैसा भय.
लताओं की तरह चढ़ता है अफसोस मेरे बदन पर.
अधपके अमरूद पेड़ से झरते हैं.

मैं जो लिखता हूं
वह एक बच्चे की अंजुलियों से रिसता हुआ पानी है.

If we could peep inside peoples' hearts,
everybody would emerge unfaithful.
Faithfulness in translation is far easier, in fact.
The picky verse doesn't sever the relationship
if there's infidelity in the translation of its obscurity.

I have the calm of ancestors.
A fear like contemporaries.
Regret climbs on my body like vines.
Unripe guavas shed from trees.

What I write
is water dripping from a child's cupped hand.

Translated by Anita Gopalan • Hindi | India

10cm
예술

나 자신: 친구들

나쁜 친구가 계속 주변을 둘러쌌으면 나는 틀림없이 감옥에 갔을 것이다. 그런데 우연인지 늘 좋은 친구들이 주변에 넘쳤다. 중학교 일학년 때 한 친구가 잠 안 오는 약을 먹고 공부하면 정말로 밤에 잠도 안 오고 공부가 잘 된다며 내게도 권했다. 그 말을 믿은 나는 그날 밤부터 약을 사 먹고 공부했다. 친구가 약을 먹고 공부하라고 했으니 약을 먹고 죽기 살기로 공부해 시험 친 과목은 모두 백 점을 맞았다. 언뜻 생각하면, 시험에서 모두 백 점을 맞으면 행복할 것 같았다. 그런데 그게 아니었다. 진짜로 허무했다. 시험 범위를 토씨 하나 안 빠뜨리고 완전히 외운 후 시험지를 받아보면 너무도 허무했다. '시시한 이놈의 세상 살기도 싫다, 뭐가 이렇게 쉬워' 하며 느끼던 실망감. 그런 허무한 감정이 폭풍처럼 지나갔다. 재미라곤 없고, 하고 싶은 일다 없었다.

친구가 책을 읽자고 해서 나는 또 죽기 살기로 읽었다. 다행히 내 친구들은 모두 좋은 아이들이어서 내가 맹목적으로 친구들의 영향을 받을 시게에 좋은 영향만 받았다.

집에서 나는 아주 성질이 나쁜 아이로 통했다. 엄마는 매일 '저거는 밖에 나가면 친구도 하나도 없겠지. 저런 아이하고 누...

10cm Art

The Real Me: Friends

There's no doubt that I would have ended up in jail if I had continued to keep bad company. But I was fortunate to have a lot of good friends. In my first year of middle school, I had a friend who took amphetamines to stay up all night studying. It worked, and she got good grades, and so she recommended that I try it too. I trusted her. I went out and bought some pills. That night I stayed up studying. The tests were a matter of life and death, and, in the end, I got a perfect score in every subject. I had thought that if I got perfect grades, I would be happy. But it wasn't like that. I felt so empty. When I got the tests back without a single mark on them, I felt so shallow. I said to myself in disappointment, "What a petty world we live in! It was too easy." The feeling washed over me like a raging storm. The experience hadn't been the least bit interesting. It hadn't made me want to do it again.

When my friend wanted to do test prep like that again, I did it too. Fortunately my friends were all good kids, because I followed them blindly in whatever they said or did, and it made me a better person.

At home, I was already known as a bad kid. My mother used to say, "If

Translated by Matt Reeck and Jeonghyun Mun • Korean | South Korea

you did that in front of your friends, who would want to play with you?" She worried a lot. When I brought home five or six friends from school, my mother would say, "I didn't think Cheom-seon had any friends." She was so thankful that I had friends that she really spoiled them, and they loved her back.

This happened when I was working a lot as an interpreter.

One day a friend of mine called. She said that all our friends had agreed to commit suicide together the next day. I said, "Great!" She was the one ordering us around. She had told me that I should go home, make sure to watch my mother carefully, think about the limits of life, then the next day after we got together, we would tell everyone what we had thought, then we would commit suicide together. I went home, looked deeply at my mother, then all night long thought about the meaning of life. All I came up with was paintings. All I wanted to do before dying was to paint a lot.

One time he got sick of wearing shoes, and so he stitched together some rags to make slippers and walked around like that.

The next day I enrolled in an art academy to study for the entrance exam to art school. The next year I started going to Hongik University. I painted like mad. That year I was chosen along with Nam-joon Park and Ufan Lee to be a national representative for the first Korean National Independent Art Show. At the time I had pretensions of being an artist. One day at some bar, Sang-yu Kim, my professor, asked us, "Which of you can buy paints with the money you've earned?"

None of us answered. We lowered our heads. Then he scolded us, "So you win some prize money, you buy paint, you go home and paint to your heart's content. You think that's painting? If you really want to be painters, first get married. Not with some fancy pants but with someone really poor. Wash diapers in ice water. When you go to the market, ask for a discount on bean sprouts. Triumph over life. And then paint your paintings. Right now you're like little parasites. You're sucking your parents dry like little parasites."

So I got married a month later. Just like he had instructed, I married a very poor man. He was a painter at school. Since he was addicted to drugs, he was always in and out of jail. He came to my exhibition. We talked a lot, and we became close. Some people thought we were siblings. And we had a lot in common: we had matted hair, we wore any old thing, and we were dedicated to living as we wanted.

In those days, a cutting-edge psychedelic band from Japan had performed in Korea, and, at the performance, my husband acted crazier than the singers on stage. He took off his shoes. He spun and twisted. He leaped and cavorted in ecstasy. Some audience members complained that he was blocking their view of the stage and they moved away. He was so passionate, so caught up in his dreams, so reckless, that once some idea took hold of him, he wouldn't let it go for anything. He always had a lot of girls around. He was attractive, and he knew it. His curly, wavy hair went down to his waist. His beard was so thick that it was hard to be sure just where his lips were. He was six feet, two inches. With his long hair swaying back and forth, when he walked down the street it looked like he was dancing. He wore frilly blouses and pants with feminine floral designs. One time he got sick of wearing shoes, and so he stitched together some rags to make slippers and walked around like that. But he didn't stop at that. Another time he took woolen socks for mountain climbing and made shoes. Walking around the streets, he told us how comfortable they were and that we should stop wearing shoes. I got close to him because I was always in and out of his studio. I painted there sometimes too.

One day he said to me, "Sleep with me."

"No."

"Why not?"

"STDs."

"My treatment's done."

"You're hardly done. You barely just finished!"

I like free-spirited people like him. More than anyone else, he had his own way of thinking. His approach to things was always very flexible, and he didn't believe in stereotypes. Just that would have been enough for me to like him as much as I did. Even though I liked the way he thought about art and literature, about history and society, he was hedonistic as well and devoted to satisfying all of his bodily needs. He didn't care if he got an STD, but I didn't want one. In this way, we were opposites. He kept asking me to sleep with him. And I always said no. We were really good friends.

Translated by Matt Reeck and Jeonghyun Mun • Korean | South Korea

Once I threw a closing party at his studio for a group show. I went with some pretty girls who were my juniors at school. There, a strange man was singing. "Oh, it's him!" I realized. After he sang a line, I yelled out, "Let's get married!" He said, "Great!" That night we slept together at a hotel. I had gotten married in less than a month from the time that my professor had told me to.

The Real Me: A Scary Woman

One day when I was in my early forties, my parents came over to my house. They went to another room, sat down with my husband, and started talking about me. I wasn't interested. After they left, my husband said to me, "You're a scary woman."

After graduating from college, my father told me that he wouldn't spend any more money on me. I said I needed to go to graduate school. This made my father even more determined. It didn't matter what he said because I couldn't put it off.

So I found a new way.

I called my younger siblings together.

"Drop out of school, you guys," I told them. "I'm going to use your monthly allowance. Not one of you has stayed up all night to study even once. None of you are overachievers, and none of you care about school. You guys don't have any ambition. Any money spent on you would be a waste of national resources. If you can read road signs and whatever bills you have to pay, then that's enough. Since you all can read and write, you should stop studying. But I'm special. If I had to give up studying now, it would hurt the nation. Dark storm clouds would gather overhead. For you, quitting school would be a real sign of patriotism."

Their jaws dropped. They sat there staring blankly at me. When my parents saw us, my father gave me tuition money without saying another word.

The night that my parents came over was the first time that my husband had heard that story. I still didn't know why they had so willingly given me the tuition money. I never once stopped to consider why I had brought my younger siblings together to speak to them like that.

My parents had told my husband that I was a scary woman, and that he should watch out. They were expressing their respect and sympathy for him because he had already lived with me for more than ten years. Even when he was unemployed, my husband always got infinite sympathy from my parents just because he was able to put up with me.

Translated by Matt Reeck and Jeonghyun Mun • Korean | South Korea

Standing in Water

I was born inside a boulder. I don't know anything about water. I have no water inside my body. No blood either. Nothing liquid at all. My body is hard. I'm a boulder. I'm standing in water. The water comes up to my neck. I dig my feet into the sandy bottom. Oysters live down there. They flip open their lids and show their pearls. I don't pay attention to things like pearls. People could eat them, for all I care. My head has risen high into the sky where the clouds are. There's a cool breeze there. My head feels cool.

The water laps gently. I stand without moving. The water laps against my body. Sometimes fish bump into me. But I don't move. I've been standing for so long that I'm barely breathing. I'm standing in water. I don't swim. I just stand there. I think that swimming is beneath human dignity. I'm *Homo erectus*. I think that it would be humiliating for me to swim around in the water like a fish. Even if the water pushes me under, even if water gets into my lungs and I'm about to die, I'd rather die than swim. I'd rather die.

Sleeping in the Sky

I fall down spread eagle and sleep in the sky. I sleep without making a bed, without using a pillow, without even a blanket. I sleep naked. And I dream. While dreaming, I toss and turn. I lift my legs and kick the sky. I turn on my side. I flop and flounce about. I roll around. Sometimes I fold up the clouds like pillows, and sometimes I spread them out like sheets. Then they cover me. I float up in the sky, I descend, I toss and turn to my heart's content, as I sleep and sleep and sleep. Once the sun comes up, I wake up.

When I open my eyes, my heart sinks when I see my dirty room. It's a filthy, dark room with mold growing. There are dead bugs lying shriveled up in the corners, and it stinks horribly. My room is like a tomb.

Translated by Matt Reeck and Jeonghyun Mun • Korean | South Korea

Morning Glories

Newly bloomed morning glories are beautiful. We saw them every morning. On the road to Asan Hospital, we would always see them blooming in the chain-link fence of the district's water purifying plant. Waiting for the left turn light to turn green, I would count the morning glories blooming through the fence. Sometimes I would exclaim, "Wow—there are seventeen today!" or "Look, look, there are more than thirty today!" But my husband was driving and would only stare straight ahead. After the light turned green, we would head to the hospital where he received treatment for about two hours. He had late-stage lung cancer.

He went in for treatment regularly, but his condition didn't improve. Even in the last stages of his cancer, he would drive to the hospital, and I would sit next to him in the passenger seat. Counting the morning glories, I would pretend that I wasn't sad at all. We always listened to music while driving. We would turn up an invigorating, happy song like Creedence Clearwater Revival's "Who'll Stop the Rain" or Simon and Garfunkel's "Cecilia" and sing along.

> When I got to the cathedral, I found a couple of people there already. On the way there, I had thought that I was the saddest person in the world, but when I got there, I decided it wasn't true.

After his treatment at the hospital, we drove back, and the blooms of the flowers would be closed. The next year, on a day when the morning glories bloomed through the chain-link fence, he died. Even though he died, the morning glories were in full bloom as always.

After burying him, I went home with my son. The next day I woke up early and went to the cathedral. It might have been two or three in the morning, I don't know, I didn't look at the clock. I put on clothes one by one and went out into the dark in the direction of the cathedral. My son was still sleeping. Passing by an overgrown acacia forest, I got scared. I had never had to walk anywhere alone. While my husband was still alive, we had always driven to Daejidong Cathedral. But since I didn't know how to drive, and my son didn't either, there was nothing to do but walk to the Kuuidong

Cathedral. It was almost too far for me to walk. I was so tired and my legs hurt so much that my body was shaking, and yet I didn't think about turning back. It was all I could do for my husband, and I had to make it to the cathedral. When something frightened me, I would recite my prayers a little louder, as though I could regain my peace of mind through the added vigor.

When I got to the cathedral, I found a couple of people there already. On the way there, I had thought that I was the saddest person in the world, but when I got there, I decided it wasn't true. I thought, "So there are a lot of people as sad as me." Kneeling next to them, and without moving, hoping to penetrate the meaning of Christ's existence, I stared lovingly into the red-tinted light of the Eucharist and prayed. There before the Eucharist, I recited prayer after prayer. But they weren't for me. I prayed to God to take care of my husband's soul. As I prayed, the windows gradually grew brighter, and it was time for dawn mass. After mass, I went home, reciting prayers one after another along the way. Then, before I knew it, the sun was shining brightly and it was day.

When I reached the area overgrown with plants, the morning glories appeared right in front of me. In the obscuring darkness of night, I had raced by them, but now the sun lit the forest and the morning glories were in glorious bloom. The first time I had passed by everything had been dark, but now all was light. As soon as I had awoken, I had robotically put on my clothes and walked the hard walk to the cathedral. But while walking home after mass, I felt more at ease. Scads of blooming morning glories had been sent from heaven to console me. It felt like a thousand angels were standing before me, blowing their trumpets, as though my husband had been delivered to God and heaven's trumpets were loudly singing to save my anguished soul. Thinking these thoughts, I walked on without rushing. But when I turned back to look at the morning glories, a bounce came to my step. Our son was at home, and I wanted to get back as soon as possible. On bright mornings, walking the road with the morning glories, walking to the cathedral and back—that was what I did for forty-nine consecutive days.

Translated by Matt Reeck and Jeonghyun Mun • Korean | South Korea

The Real Him: Marriage

When his excitement died down, he looked again at her. Looking at her up close, he saw that she wasn't that scary. In time, he gradually saw that she was more sincere and innocent than everyone else. Then, after more days had passed, he spoke up, "If I get a place somewhere, will you come too?"

"Of course," the scary woman answered. "Why do you even ask? We're married, aren't we?"

But he wasn't able to find a place. Not being able to wait, she wrote home. Her parents sent money, and she found them a place. So they started living together.

A Buddha in the Water's Depths

I don't have gills. And I don't know how to swim. Rather than learn how to swim, I would rather go to a laboratory to invent gills. Then when I lower myself into the water's depths, I would put these gills in my nose and mouth, and I would breathe.

Someone is sitting in the water's depths. He is breathing freely. He has gills. He is meditating in the water's depths. He can hear the wind blowing above the water. He can feel the wave in the water caused by the movements of fish. He can feel the water plants growing. He is sitting there in the water's depths quite comfortably. He is sitting there motionlessly while the water passes by. His hair is standing on end like antennae pointing in every which direction. Even though he can feel every movement in the water, he's relaxed. Even nearby movements can't disturb his meditation. He's completely free.

Translated by Matt Reeck and Jeonghyun Mun • Korean | South Korea

The Rising Sun in the Glass of Water

There is a glass of water on my desk. It's full of water. The sun is rising in the water. I look at the glass. I stare at the rising sun. I can't make up my mind. Should I swallow the water, or should I pour it out really fast?

I reach out and grab the glass. I slowly put it to my lips. I drink it in one gulp.

But what's that now? The water is still there. The sun is still there. Now a thunderstorm rages in my stomach. Not the sort of parasite happy simply to follow food through the body, it burrows somewhere in my intestinal wall. It's that sort of sun. It's looking for something. There it is—the heart! That's where the sun always rises.

I'm looking at the glass with the sun inside, the glass on my desk. I'm looking at the rising sun encased in a heart in my glass of water. The heart is the sun's hometown. That's where the sun was born.

A Hundred Suns

One morning I climbed to the top of a mountain. I saw the rising sun. There was only one sun rising over the mountain. It brought tears to my eyes. I grew angry. Why is there only one sun?

It's boring to have only one sun. There should be a sun that rises from the east, from the north, and from the west. There should be a sun that rises next to the mountain in the east where the sun rises, and many suns in a row rising after the first. I don't want to live in a world with only one rising sun. I hate things of which there is only one in the world. It makes me nauseous when people worship something for being the only one of its kind. The sun gets too much credit. It's because there's only one of them. To make the idiots shut up, O, sun, please, hundreds of you rise together!

Translated by Matt Reeck and Jeonghyun Mun • Korean | South Korea

The Person Who Walked Hugging a Bird

There was an artist living alone on a desolate beach. He had a sullen disposition. He never spoke to the people living in the nearby village. He had no dealings with them at all. But one brave girl would take walks on the beach. Large birds lived there too. One day there was a typhoon. One of the birds got injured. The sullen artist who had no sympathy for humans looked at the bird and cried. He didn't know how to help it, and so he just sat there and cried. But the girl was walking on the beach, and she saw what had happened. She took the injured bird back to her house and treated its wounds. After a while, the bird got better. When it was completely healed, she took it back to the beach. This was when the artist spoke to the girl for the first time. The two of them helped it take flight.

This is the plot of a short story I read a long time ago. It has stayed with me, and sometimes I find myself painting a person carrying a bird. Sometimes I draw a person carrying a fish. I keep drawing a person carrying something. Sometimes I am the person carrying something, and sometimes I am the bird or the fish getting carried. I change subjects every now and then.

Birds live on land. Fish are from an entirely different world. Sometimes people treat the beasts of land with compassion, and sometimes they love animals from different worlds. Right now a woman holding a dog is walking by.

Even before I went to art school, I used to draw pictures of the girl carrying the bird all by herself. When I painted her for the second time, she became a motif for me—the girl carrying the bird. The first time I thought of her was when I was looking in a magazine at a small black and white photograph of the castle where the Renaissance thinker Montaigne lived. It had three floors. The first floor was the dining room, the second was the bedroom, and the third was the study. It was a house fit for one. A turret. He lived there alone. From his windows, he looked out over the farmers in their fields and wrote and wrote and lived and died. I wanted to live like that. Because I wanted to have his life, I painted that picture and stuck it on the wall. Then I got sad because it wasn't my house. Every day I lamented the fact that I wasn't Montaigne.

I really wanted to live a simple life like Montaigne's. No roaches in my room, none in the kitchen, the breeze blowing gently through the windows,

a rough blanket in my bedroom, a book I want to read in my study. My bathroom, my dining room...a quiet, simple life. That was the life I dreamed of.

Translated by Matt Reeck and Jeonghyun Mun • Korean | South Korea

Contributors

MARILYN BOOTH is the Khalid bin Abdullah Al Saud Professor for the Study of the Contemporary Arab World at the Oriental Institute and Magdalen College of Oxford University. She has been Senior Humanities Research Fellow, New York University Abu Dhabi, and Iraq Professor of Arabic and Islamic Studies at the University of Edinburgh. She has translated numerous novels, short story collections, and memoirs from Arabic, most recently two novels by Lebanese novelist Hassan Daoud, *The Penguin's Song* (City Lights Publishers, 2015) and *No Road to Paradise* (American University in Cairo Press, 2017), winner of the Naguib Mahfouz Medal for Literature.

ANITA GOPALAN is a 2016 PEN/Heim Translation Fund Grant recipient for her translation of *Simsim* by Geet Chaturvedi. She graduated in computer science and mathematics from BITS Pilani, and worked in the banking and technology sectors in India, Australia, New Zealand, Singapore, and the Middle East. Her work has appeared or is forthcoming in *World Literature Today*, *Poetry International Rotterdam*, *Modern Poetry in Translation*, *Drunken Boat*, *91st Meridian*, and elsewhere. A translator and artist, she lives in Bangalore.

MARILYN HACKER is the author of thirteen books of poems, including *A Stranger's Mirror* (W. W. Norton, 2015), *Names* (W. W. Norton, 2010), and *Desesperanto* (W. W. Norton, 2003); an essay collection, *Unauthorized Voices* (University of Michigan Press, 2010); and fourteen collections of translations of French and Francophone poets including Emmanuel Moses, Marie Étienne, Vénus Khoury-Ghata, Habib Tengour, and Rachida Madani. *Diaspo/Renga*, a collaborative sequence written with Deema Shehabi, was published in 2014. Her awards include the Lenore Marshall Poetry Prize in 1995 for *Winter Numbers*, two Lambda Literary Awards, the 2009 American PEN Award for Poetry in Translation, the 2010 PEN/Voelcker Award, and the international Argana Prize for Poetry from the Beit as-Sh'ir/House of Poetry in Morocco in 2011. She lives in Paris.

DIMITER KENAROV is a freelance journalist, poet, and translator. He is the author of two collections of Bulgarian poetry and a book of translations of the selected poems of Elizabeth Bishop. His English-language poetry and poetry translations from Bulgarian have appeared in *The American Poetry Review*, *The Gettysburg Review*, *The New England Review*, and *Poetry International*, among others.

JONATHAN LARSON is a poet and translator living in Brooklyn. Recent work has appeared or is forthcoming in *Asymptote*, *Black Sun Lit*, *The Brooklyn Rail*, *Gulf Coast*, and *Lana Turner* among others. A translation of Francis Ponge's *Nioque of the Early Spring* will be published in 2017 by Red Dust Books. Jonathan teaches in the German Department at New York University.

JI YOON LEE is a poet and translator, most recently of *Cheer Up, Femme Fatale* by Kim Yiduen (Action Books, 2015). She is the author of *Foreigner's Folly* (Coconut Books, 2014), *FunSize/BiteSize* (Birds of Lace, 2013), and *IMMA* (Radioactive Moat Press, 2012). She is the winner of the Joanna Cargill Prize (2014) and finalist for the 1913 First Book Prize (2012). Poems and translations have appeared in *Asymptote*, *Eleven Eleven*, *The Volta*, *PANK*, *Bambi Muse*, *Seven Corners*, *The Animated Reader*, *&Now Awards 3*, and more. She received her MFA in creative writing from the University of Notre Dame.

JAKE LEVINE is a poet and translator. He edits for Spork Press and is getting his PhD at Seoul National University in comparative literature. His translation of Kim Kyung Ju's *I Am a Season That Does Not Exist in the World* (Black Ocean, 2015) was a finalist for the ALTA Lucien Stryk Prize for Translation.

CHRISTINA MACSWEENEY was awarded the 2016 Valle Inclán Translation Prize for her translation of Valeria Luiselli's *The Story of My Teeth*. She has published two other books by the same author, and her translations of Daniel Saldaña París's novel *Among Strange Victims*, and Eduardo Rabasa's *A Zero-Sum Game* both appeared in 2016. She has also published translations, articles, and interviews on a wide variety of platforms, including *Words Without Borders*, *Music & Literature*, *Literary Hub*, and *BOMB* magazine, plus in the anthologies *México20*, *Lunatics, Lovers and Poets: Twelve Stories after Cervantes and Shakespeare*, and *Crude Words: Contemporary Writing from Venezuela*. She is currently working on texts by the Mexican authors Julián Herbert and Verónica Gerber Bicecci.

ERIKA MIHÁLYCSA is a lecturer in twentieth-century British literature at Babeş-Bolyai University, Cluj, Romania. She has translated works by Samuel Beckett, Flann O'Brien, Anne Carson, Patrick McCabe, and others into Hungarian, and published short prose in both Hungarian and English. She is the editor of *Hyperion: On the Future of Aesthetics* (Contra Mundum Press). Her translations of contemporary Hungarian literature have appeared in *World Literature Today*, *Two Lines*, *Trafika Europe*, *Music & Literature*, *Envoi*, and elsewhere.

JEONGHYUN MUN graduated from Sungkyunkwan University, with a major in Korean language and literature, and the University of Waterloo, receiving honors in economics. She teaches in the Korean and English Translation and Interpretation Program at King George International College in Toronto.

SIMON PARE is British and lives in Paris. He translates literature, nonfiction, and film from German and French. His published translations include works by the Austrian author Christoph Ransmayr and French-Algerian author Anouar Benmalek as well as the English edition of *The Panama Papers*. An excerpt from *With Your Hands* by Ahmed Kalouaz appeared in *Two Lines 20: Landmarks*.

ONDREJ PAZDIREK is a translator and a poet. He grew up in Prague, Czech Republic, and moved to the U.S. at the age of eighteen. He holds an MA in poetry from the University of Cincinnati. His translations of Kamil Bouška, from Czech, have previously appeared in *Guernica* and *B O D Y*. His own poems have been published in *Bayou Magazine*, *Radar Poetry*, and *Euphony*.

MATT REECK has translated from French, Hindi, Korean, and Urdu. He has been awarded a Fulbright Fellowship, a PEN/Heim Translation Fund Grant, and an NEA Literary Translation Fellowship.

ROBERT S. RUDDER taught Spanish at the University of Minnesota during the 1960s, where he met Ana María Matute and translated some of her stories. Later, while teaching at UCLA and other universities, his translations of *Lazarillo de Tormes*, and of such writers as Benito Pérez Galdós, Rosario Castellanos, and Cristina Peri Rossi were published. He has received writing grants from the Spanish Ministry of Culture, and the National Endowment for the Arts.

RICHARD SIEBURTH has translated works by Nostradamus, Maurice Scève, Louise Labé, Friedrich Hölderlin, Georg Büchner, Gershom Scholem, Walter Benjamin, Gérard de Nerval, Henri Michaux, Antonin Artaud, Guillevic, and Michael Palmer. He has also edited a number of Ezra Pound's works, including *A Walking Tour in Southern France*, *The Pisan Cantos*, *Poems & Translations*, and *New Selected Poems and Translations*. His *Late Baudelaire* is forthcoming from Yale University Press.

JEREMY TIANG has translated more than ten books from Chinese, including novels by Chan Ho-Kei, Wang Jinkang, Yeng Pway Ngon, and Zhang Yueran, and has received a PEN/Heim Translation Fund Grant and an NEA Literary Translation Fellowship. He also writes and translates plays. Jeremy's short story collection *It Never Rains on National Day* (Epigram Books, 2015) was a finalist for the Singapore Literature Prize.

Credits

AL-HARTHI, JOKHA

"Wardat Maymuna." *Majallat al-Dawha*, no. 85 (November 2014). Printed with permission from the author. All rights reserved.

BICECCI, VERÓNICA GERBER

Excerpt from *Conjunto vacío*. Mexico City: Almadía Ediciones S.A.P.I. de C.V., 2015. "Empty Set" printed with permission from Coffee House Press. All rights reserved.

BOUŠKA, KAMIL

"Konfese," Sirény," and "Slavnost" from *Oheň po slavnosti*. Prague: Fra, 2011.

CHATURVEDI, GEET

"Khushiyon Ke Guptachar" and "Biodata." *Sabad* (April 2016). "Maalik Ko Khush Karne Ke Liye Kisi Bhi Seema Tak Jaane Wala Maanviya Dimagh Aur Apni Nasl Ka Shuruaati Joota" from *Aalaap Mein Girah*. New Delhi: Rajkamal Prakashan, 2010. "Doodh Ke Daant" from *Nyoontam Main*. New Delhi: Rajkamal Prakashan, 2017.

ILKOV, ANI

"Tehnika" and "Vita nuova" from *Etymologicals*. Plovdiv, Bulgaria: Zhanet 45, 1996. "Kammeni vaglishta" from *Love of Nature*. Plovdiv, Bulgaria: Hristo G. Danov, 1989.

KIM, CHEOM-SEON

"Na chasin: chhinkudeul," "Na chasin: Museoun nyeon," "Mul sokeseo seo itda," "haeuleseo chamchanda," "Naphalkkot," "Keu chasin: Kyeorheon," "Mul sokeui bucheo," "Yurikheup sokeseo ddeuneun hae," "Baek kaeeui thaeyang," and "saereul anko kaneun saram" from *10cm yaesul*. Seoul: Maum Sanchek, 2002.

KIM, MIN JEONG

"Ppalgange Gohada," "Peniseuraneun Ireumui Jot," and "Pinalle" from *Geunyeo-ga Cheoeum Neukkigi Sijakaetda*. Seoul: Moonji Press, 2015.

LANGE-MÜLLER, KATJA

Excerpt from *Verfrühte Tierliebe*. Cologne, Germany: Verlag Kiepenheuer & Witsch GmbH & Co. KG © 1995. All rights reserved.

MATUTE, ANA MARÍA

"El bosque" from *Tres y un sueño*. Barcelona: Ediciones Destino © 1961, Herederos de Ana María Matute. All rights reserved.

MAYRÖCKER, FRIEDERIKE

"ich öffne weinend die Tür und es fällt mir vor die Füsze : fällt...," "An.," "der lächelnde weisze Schwan auf dem weißen Badetuch = Scardanelli Version," and "dann hört alles plötzlich auf auch die Lerche Narzisse die..." from *Scardanelli*. Berlin: Suhrkamp, 2009.

MICHAUX, HENRI

"Naissance," "Première mort de Plume," and "Deuxième mort de Plume" from *Un Certain Plume*. Paris: Editions du Carrefour, 1930.

NEGROUCHE, SAMIRA

"Nœuds en zigzag" from *Six arbres de fortune autour de ma baignoire*. Plaisir: Éditions Mazette, 2017.

TAKÁCS, ZSUZSA

"A test feltámadása" from *A megtévesztő külsejű vendég. Önéletrajzaim*. Budapest: Magvető, 2007.

YAN, GE

"Beishang Shou" from *Yishou Zhi*. Beijing: CITIC Publishing Group, 2006.

Index by Language